STRANGE WITNESS

REVENGE: a seven letter word that stood for every year that Hart Jackson had spent in jail. The moment of his release, Jackson went straight for Flip Evans who had framed him. In a heart-stopping trail across Chicago, Jackson became entangled with a gang of cold-blooded killers. If Flip's gang didn't get him first, the cops would.

DAY KEENE

◆

STRANGE WITNESS

Complete and Unabridged

397027

LINFORD
Leicester

First published in the
United States of America in 1970 by
Macfadden-Bartell Corporation
New York

First Linford Edition
published August 1991

British Library CIP Data

Keene, Day
    Strange witness. — Large print ed. —
    Linford mystery library
    I. Title
    813.54 [F]

    ISBN 0–7089–7078–8

Published by
F. A. Thorpe (Publishing) Ltd.
Anstey, Leicestershire

Set by Words & Graphics Ltd.
Anstey, Leicestershire
Printed and bound in Great Britain by
T. J. Press (Padstow) Ltd., Padstow, Cornwall

1

DURING the night Spring tiptoed north. The sun felt hotter than it had. Green shoots sprouted in the fields. An early returning robin surveyed the scene from the budding limb of a great oak tree rising out of the prison yard.

Hart Jackson eyed the robin as the guard unlocked the big front gate. "Better take off, fellow."

The gate guard grinned. "You don't think much of our hospitality, eh, Jackson?"

A big man with a slightly twisted smile, Jackson filled his lungs with air. On the far side of the wall, even the air was different. "That's for sure, bud," he told the guard. "Unfortunately, I'll be back."

The guard's grin faded. "Nix, now. Don't talk like that."

The reply appeared to come from the bright-eyed robin. It cocked its head on one side and asked, "Okay. How do you want me to talk? How would you feel if some bastard had you tucked away for seven years?"

The guard took off his cap and wiped the leather sweat band as he looked from the bird to Hart. The big man's lips were compressed and motionless. "You're good, man," the guard admitted.

Hart lit a cigarette. "At least I used to be."

He stood a moment studying the prison parking lot. No one had come to meet him. He hadn't expected to be met. There was no one left who cared. He picked up his heavy cowhide bags. "Well, *hasta la vista*."

"What does that mean?" the guard asked.

Hart Jackson told him. "Until we meet again."

There was a bus stop on the corner. Jackson walked toward it slowly, savoring the air. Seven years was a long time.

He could expect a lot of changes. He had a slight feeling of unreality. Only his sense of injustice was real. After spending seven years in a cell, only his hate for Flip Evans was normal. The robin had named Flip Evans correctly. The fat man was a bastard.

Jackson rolled a cigarette as he waited for the bus, wondering what it would be like to smoke a cigar again, the kind he once had smoked. An off-duty guard joined the small group around the bus sign.

The guard nodded pleasantly. "Leaving us, eh, Jackson?"

"So it would seem," Jackson said.

He fingered the five dollar bill in his pocket, tempted. He didn't *have* to go back to Chicago. He looked at the expensive watch on his wrist. He could hock his watch and the stuff in his bags for enough to buy a plane ticket to L.A. He hadn't lost his talent. He was still a good showman. He'd paid his alleged debt to society. He could start life all over again on the coast. In time he might even marry.

Sweat beaded his forehead at the thought. Seven years was a long time for a man to go without a woman. He tried to put the thought out of his mind and failed as a well-dressed girl joined the group at the bus sign. Jackson eyed her surreptitiously. The girl was young and blonde and vibrant, the type of girl he had once known. For a moment he thought she was going to speak. She didn't.

Jackson continued to watch her as she waited for the bus that would take him into town and decided that the girl had troubles of her own. Her man was probably in Stateville. She'd probably just come from her monthly visit through wire mesh, a hopeless, meaningless visit leaving them both in physical and mental torment. He was glad no one had come to see him.

The off-duty guard tried to be friendly. "Made any plans, Jackson?"

"No. Not as yet," Jackson lied.

"The boys are going to miss you."

4

"I suppose."

Jackson was glad when the bus came and he no longer had to look at the girl. She rode in one of the front seats, only the crown of her straw-colored hair visible. He rode, caressing it with his eyes. A man got off the bus. A woman carrying a child got on.

The off-duty guard continued trying to be friendly. "Mind if I say something, fellow?"

"Not at all," Jackson assured him.

The guard eyed the big man's once expensive suit and topcoat. "We don't get many like you in Stateville," he said finally. "Most of the guys we handle deserve to be in the jug. You're different. You're a gentleman. You're used to making a lot of dough, making it on the legit, too. How much you used to draw in a week, Jackson?"

Jackson thought a moment. "I got twenty-five hundred at Chez Paree, but I'd say I averaged around a thousand."

The guard whistled softly. "That's fifty-two thousand bucks a year, three times as much as the warden makes."

"So?"

The guard laid his hand on Jackson's knee. "So, don't come back, fellow. Sure. I know how you feel. You think you got a bum deal. You're so filled with hate that it's running out of your ears." He continued earnestly. "But so you do something about it. Who do you hurt? Yourself."

Jackson sucked at his hand-rolled cigarette wishing it was a cigar. "Why all the interest in me?"

The guard told him. "Because I like you. Because all the guards liked you during the time you've been with us. Because we think you're a square-shooter. Because I heard what you made the 'robin' tell the gate guard. So Flip Evans is a bastard. Uh uh. Don't do it, Jackson."

Jackson's voice was small and infantile from the lips of the baby in the arms of the woman across the aisle. "Okay. I'll tell him when he comes in."

The woman gasped. "My God! Did

you hear my baby talk?"

The guard shrugged and read his paper.

Hart continued to watch the crown of blond hair showing over the top of the front seat.

The Greyhound bus station was crowded. The next bus for Chicago didn't leave for half an hour. Hart Jackson bought a ticket and still carrying the heavy bags, walked into the washroom. An attendant filled a bowl with water and laid a clean towel beside it. Jackson studied his face as he washed.

His eyes were clear. There was a little more gray in his black hair than there had been, but his face had lost its nightclub pallor. He'd even put on a little weight. Physically, prison had been good for him. For seven years he'd kept regular hours, eaten at specified times, slept or tried to sleep a stipulated number of hours. His clothes though slightly outmoded were still smart and expensive looking. He didn't even look as if he'd been in prison. Only the dark shadows under his eyes showed his mental turmoil.

To kill Flip Evans or not? That was the question.

Hate wasn't something a man got over in minutes. Not when he'd lived with it for years. Then there were Helene and Jerry to consider. Killing Flip would be a monument to them. Men like Flip never changed. As long as he lived he would continue to ruin other lives, spread his insidious poison. Jackson flipped a mental coin and still could come to no decision.

"I don't know. I'll be damned if I know," he told his reflection.

He tipped the attendant a quarter, picked up his bags and walked back to the waiting room. It was nice just to be with people again, people free to come and go as they pleased. Man wasn't conditioned to be cooped up like an animal. It did something to him, especially if he'd been unjustly imprisoned.

The girl at the cigar counter was sorry.

The best cigars she had were her three for a dollar brand. Jackson bought six of them with his last two dollars and lit one gratefully. It tasted good. If he followed the guard's advice he could continue to smoke good cigars. So his debt had been unowed; he'd paid it. Thirty-five wasn't old. A man at thirty-five was in the prime of life. The world was wide. He was free to go where he pleased.

He looked for the blond girl and found her. She was waiting at the Number 4 ramp. She, too, was bound for Chicago. Jackson stood enjoying his cigar, admiring her. She was, he judged, in her early or middle twenties. Her stomach was concave. She was slim flanked and full breasted. Her legs were long and shapely. There was an aura of health about her. She looked as if at one time she might have been a farm girl. But that had been some time ago. Now her eyes were too old for her face. She had that certain brittle look. Her gray flannel suit had cost plenty. So had her silver fox fur.

Jackson realized he was sweating again. He realized the girl was smiling at him. Then a new and sobering thought struck him. Flip Evans knew he was getting out. The fat man had to know. What if Flip had sent the girl as a lure? God knew she was pretty enough to tempt any man to follow her anywhere.

He closed his eyes and tried to remember from what direction she had come. It hadn't been from the direction of the prison. She'd crossed the street to the bus stop. It could well be that she'd been waiting in a car for him to appear. He tried to remember if there had been a car and couldn't. At the time it hadn't mattered.

Jackson rolled his cigar between his lips. He had to know. It might help him make his decision. If Evans was still gunning for him, he had no choice. He picked up his bags and walked over to where the girl was standing.

"Haven't we met before?"

The girl appraised him slowly. Her breasts rose and fell with her breathing.

"Why, no, I don't believe we have." She wet her lips with her tongue. "But if you're who I think you are, it could be arranged."

"Who do you think I am?"

It was a question. "Hart Jackson?"

"That's right," Jackson said coldly.

The girl's fingers bit into his arm. "Then I have to talk to you. I came all the way down to meet you when you got out. Then I wasn't certain it was you." Her eyes bored into his. "You looked too handsome, too distinguished to have spent seven years in prison. Then when I saw you talking to that guard, I thought you were an official of some kind and lost my nerve."

Jackson was grimly amused. The kid was good. "I see."

Her eyes continued to search his face. "You can prove you are Hart Jackson?"

The mouth of the head of her silver fox fur formed the clasp that held the fur together. Jackson took the head in one hand and made the mouth open and close with his fingers.

"You tell 'em, sister," the fox head seemed to say.

The girl laughed in relief. "You're Jackson, all right. They told me you were clever, but I didn't realize how clever. And you are nice, as nice as I knew you would be."

Jackson removed her hand from his arm and shook his head. "Uh uh."

The girl's eyes clouded. "Uh uh, what?"

Jackson told her. "It won't work, sister."

"What won't work?"

"What you're trying to pull." Jackson picked up his bags again as the public address system announced the Chicago bus. "It isn't bad bait. It's nice. I'd like to nibble. But the price is much too high."

He walked on up the ramp. As he boarded the bus, he looked back over his shoulder. The girl was still standing where he'd left her. Her lips were quivering as if she were about to cry. Then the surge of the crowd pushed him forward. He didn't know if she got on the bus or not. He didn't care.

The long ride through the fallow countryside seemed endless. Jackson rode staring out of the window, rolling his dead cigar between his lips, trying not to think of the girl. It would have been nice if it could have been different. He was glad when the greening fields dropped behind and the big bus rolled down city streets again. He was ready and waiting at the door when the bus stopped. The girl had gotten on the bus. She disembarked quickly behind him and attempted to catch his arm.

"Hart, please," she begged him. "You have to listen to me."

He shrugged her hand off his arm. "Sorry," he said curtly and carrying his bags he walked swiftly out of the crowded terminal into equally crowded Randolph Street.

It felt good to be back in Chicago. It hadn't changed in the seven years he'd been gone, at least not appreciably. Its skyscrapers were just as tall. The wind whistled around the corners. The girls were just as pretty.

Jackson walked west on Randolph to Dearborn, then north on Dearborn across the river. There were still ice cakes in the river. Spring wasn't apparent in the city as it had been in the farm land.

He passed a pawn shop then another then two more before he came to the one he wanted. It was smaller than the ones he'd passed. The merchandise displayed in the window was cheaper. Jackson turned in without stopping and set his heavy bags on the counter under the printed legend — *PLEDGES*.

The old man back of the counter eyed the bags without interest. "Yeah? So what can I do for you, mister?"

Jackson told him. "I want to pawn both bags and their contents. And I want to buy a gun, preferably a short barreled .38."

The old man opened the bag nearest him and took out a ventriloquist's dummy. "Uh uh," he shook his head. "Sure, I know. It cost a lot of dough. But I can't

14

lend you a dime on it. You gotta know how to use those things." He opened the second bag, unfolded the evening clothes it contained and glanced respectfully at the labels. There was sincere regret in his voice this time. "That goes for the soup and the fish and the dinner jacket." He raised his heavy lidded eyes to Jackson's. "Besides, I don't sell guns."

Jackson nodded. "Okay." He peeled his watch from his wrist and laid it on the counter. "To hell with the clothes and the dummy. The bags are worth two hundred apiece. I'll take fifty for them and five hundred on the watch."

The old man picked up the watch and examined it under a jeweler's glass. "Say four hundred," he bargained.

Jackson countered, "Five for both the bags and the watch."

The dummy on the counter sat up suddenly and peered intently into the pawnbroker's face while its grinning lips advised, "Don't be an umpchay, mister. Profit is where you find it." The dummy craned its neck around the store as if to make certain it wasn't being overheard then leaned forward again and whispered in the old man's ear, "Besides, Whitey told us you did sell guns to right guys." The dummy winked at Jackson. "Didn't he, Obnoxious?"

The pawnbroker looked from the dummy to Jackson. An unlighted cigar in his mouth, Jackson's lean lips hadn't moved. Belated recognition lighted the old man's face.

"Oh. Yeah. Sure. I know who you are now. When did you get out, fellow?"

"This morning," Jackson told him,.

The old man returned their contents to the bags and picked the watch from the counter.

"Okay. Let's go in the back room. I think we can work out something."

2

OUTSIDE the pawn shop again, Jackson walked slowly back down Clark Street toward the Loop. North Clark Street hadn't changed. There was a bar on every corner. Most of them advertised some strip or topless attraction. The windows of the nightclubs and the bars were still filled with pictures of pretty girls in various stages of undress.

He studied several of the windows. None of the girls were as pretty as the little blonde whom Flip had sent to intercept him. He wondered just what her game had been, probably to lure him to some hotel room or apartment where the Deacon or some other one of Flip's boys was waiting.

He walked on with his hand on the butt of the gun in his pocket. The gun itself was a violation of his parole. If he were picked up with a gun on his

17

person, he would be sent back to sweat out the full twenty years. He hadn't thought of that. The thought caused his stomach to turn over. He'd had all he wanted of prison. If he went back to Stateville again, it wouldn't be to do time.

He felt suddenly naked and exposed. The first cop who recognized him might well frisk him for luck and Flip would have won again without even lifting a finger. He wasn't being smart. He was acting like a chump. He was allowing his hate to dull his mind. There was nothing he could do for hours but wait. It would be impossible for him to get into Flip's penthouse apartment. And Flip never showed at the Club until midnight.

The wind seemed suddenly colder than it had been and raw. There was a hotel and bar on the next corner. As Jackson neared it, a newspaper truck dropped off a bundle of early evening papers at the newsstand on the corner. Jackson bought a paper and turned into the bar. Being in a bar was another violation of his parole, but at least he was off the street. He'd buy a few drinks, he decided, then get a room and lie low until midnight.

Early as it was, a B girl sat down beside him. "Lonely, honey?"

"Not particularly," Jackson told her.

She squirmed closer to him. "How's for being a good sport and buying me a drink anyway?"

The smell of her cheap perfume sickened Jackson. He bought her a drink to get rid of her then read the paper to kill time. The paper headlined the disappearance of one Fillmore Pierce. Jackson vaguely remembered the name then placed it. Pierce was the aging playboy heir to the Pierce packing money. He started to read the story then noticed an item datelined Joliet and read about himself instead. The item read;

JOLIET — Hart Jackson, former well-known ventriloquist and nightclub entertainer, was released from Stateville

Prison this morning after serving seven years of a twenty-year sentence for murder. Still maintaining his innocence of the crime, Jackson stated that while his plans for the future had been formulated, he would rather not make them public at the present time. Convicted and sentenced in 1963 for the so-called 'penthouse' murder of Helene Adele, beautiful blues singer of the swank Club Bali, Jackson was . . .

Feeling a slight pressure on his knee, without looking up, Jackson said, "Go away. I bought you a drink. I told you I wasn't lonely."

Then he knew even before he looked. The perfume was different. It was clean and fresh and wholesome. "Where'd you come from?" he asked the blonde.

She said, "I followed you. In a cab. From the bus station."

Jackson was almost afraid to look over his shoulder. "Alone? What's the idea?"

"I told you. I want to talk to you."

"About what?"

"About us."

Jackson noticed for the first time that her lower lip was quivering and that her makeup was streaked as if she had been crying. He shook his head. "I don't get it."

She said, "Suppose I told you that I know Flip Evans framed you in the Helene Adele killing?"

"How could you know?"

"Suppose Flip told me."

Jackson looked at her with new interest. "Would you be willing to put that in writing?"

"I would." The girl's eyes searched his face. "On one condition."

"What's that?"

"That you marry me. Now. Right now. Today."

Jackson took off his hat and ran his fingers through his hair. Then he signaled the bartender. "Another double rye for me. And whatever the lady is drinking."

The barman started to say something and changed his mind. "Okay, fellow. A double rye for you. And a Scotch and soda for Miss Winston."

Jackson was amused. "He seems to know you."

The blonde said wryly, "A lot of people know me. And the first name, if you're interested, is Thelma."

Jackson played along to learn her game. "I'm glad to know you, Thelma. Now, what was that you said?"

The girl repeated, "I'm willing to swear to anything, do anything you say, if you'll marry me."

"Oh, yes. Right now. Today."

"That's right."

Jackson felt as if a tight band were drawn around his head shutting off all circulation. One of them had to be crazy. Still, the only sign of a possible mental disturbance was the girl's twitching lips. He said, "As I recall, there is a slight matter of a license before a marriage can be performed."

The girl took a paper from her purse and spread it on the bar. "I have one. I got one yesterday." Her lips continued to twitch as she laid a roll of bills on top of the license. "What's more, I'll give you five hundred dollars down and there'll be more money later. In fact, ten thousand more."

"This isn't a gag?" Jackson asked.

"No, I've never been more serious."

A passing truck backfired and the girl winced. She was obviously frightened. But some emotion greater than her fear was driving her. Jackson suddenly felt sorry for her. He laid a big hand on the small one on the bar.

"Okay. So why do you want to marry me?"

The girl's voice was low and throaty. "Don't ask me how I know, but you're a right guy, Jackson." Her wet eyes searched his face. "The kind of guy I used to think I'd fall in love with. A man who fights for what he knows is right — a man who takes care of his own."

Jackson squeezed the hand under his. "So why not tell me the story?"

She shook her head. "I can't. Not here.

It's too long. But I'll tell you as soon as we're married. I want you to know." She paused, then added, "And you'd better let me put that gun you're carrying in my bag. Remember you're only out on parole."

Jackson removed his hand from the small one on the bar. He felt cheated, put upon. He'd been on the verge of believing the girl, believing that, screwball as it sounded, she had some reason for wanting to marry him. The kid was a capable actress. She'd almost had him fooled. She didn't want him. All she wanted was his gun, the gun with which he intended to kill Flip.

He shook his head. "Uh uh. I'll take a chance on being picked up."

"But you will marry me?"

Jackson was suddenly tired. He'd never been so tired. It was the first time he'd ever heard of a professional beauty being hired to propose marriage as a lure. He had no doubt she would lead him straight to Evans. But that was all right with him. Evans was the man he wanted to see.

24

He called her bluff. "Okay. Let's go get married."

Jackson's feeling of unreality continued. This couldn't be happening to him. In a minute the bell would ring and he'd wake up back in Stateville in his cell. He had to be dreaming this. He had to.

The parsonage parlor was small. A smell of frying onions filled the building. The young minister's voice droned on:

" . . . authority committed unto me as a Minister of The Church, I declare that Hart Johnson and Thelma Winston are now husband and wife, according to the ordinance of God and the law of this State, in the name of the Father and the Son and the Holy Spirit. Amen."

Crying even harder than she had been the blonde girl lifted her lips to be kissed. Jackson kissed her as a matter of form then gave the young minster a bill from the roll he'd gotten by hocking his watch.

The minister, in turn, wished them every happiness and escorted them to the door. Jackson stood on the stoop a moment in the growing dusk of early evening cupping his hands against the rising wind as he lighted a cigar.

His new wife wiped her tears with a wisp of a handkerchief. "I won't cry any more," she promised. "Now, do you believe me?"

Jackson helped her down the steps. He'd never been as puzzled. "Well, you went through with it," he admitted. "So what happens now?"

The blonde girl met his eyes. "Whatever you want to happen. I meant every word I said. I want to be your wife in every sense."

"You have an apartment?"

"I have. But I'd rather not go there."

"Why not?"

"You'll know when I tell you. Why don't we check into a hotel?"

"You mean that?"

"I do."

"What hotel?"

"You still don't trust me, do you, Hart?"

"No."

"You have to," she insisted, as she kissed him.

Jackson tried to hate the girl and couldn't. It had been seven years since he had held a woman in his arms. Her body was soft and yielding. The tired look left her eyes.

"Trust me. Believe in me, Hart" she pleaded.

Her right hand left his shoulder and dipped into the pocket of his coat just as he heard and saw the car. The Deacon was leaning out the window, a blank, business-like automatic in his hand.

"Hi, fellow," the Deacon said coldly.

Jackson swore under his breath. "I knew it. Why, you dirty little Judas!" He slapped the blonde girl away from him and dove for the gun she'd dropped on the grass just as the car, driven by Flip Evans, drew abreast of where they were standing. The girl's suddenly out-thrust foot sent him sprawling on the parsonage lawn as the Deacon opened fire. As he fell he heard Evans shout:

"No. Get out of the way, you little fool. Get — "

The door of the parsonage opened. A man began to shout. A police whistle shrilled on the corner and a not distant radio car siren answered it. The man in the car stopped shooting. The big car whipped in a sharp U-turn and disappeared in the deepening dusk.

His hands and knees sodden with mud, Jackson got to his feet cursing — then stopped short. He knew why Thelma had thrown away his gun. He knew why she had tripped him. He knew why Evans had shouted. The blonde girl hadn't wanted him to be killed and after tripping him, she had deliberately shielded his body with her own.

She lay on the muddy grass between the sidewalk and the curb, blood staining her white blouse. Hart knelt beside her and took her in his arms.

"I — I meant to, Hart," she whispered. "And I didn't mean this to happen. I — I didn't know I'd been followed."

Hart held her a little tighter. "I believe

you." The siren was louder now. "Now, don't even take a deep breath until an ambulance gets here."

She shook her head. "I have to talk. It's up to you, now."

"What's up to me?"

"To take care of Olga." A spasm of pain racked her. "She's at the Logan Square Hotel. In Room 410,"

The first police car braked at the curb.

"What goes here?" a patrolman demanded.

Jackson told him. "My wife has been shot."

3

THE nightmare had been going on for hours. Jackson had no doubt it would continue. The light shining in his eyes had ceased to be a light. It was a needle-pointed gimlet of pain boring ever deeper into his brain. He wished he knew if Thelma was still alive. The last he'd heard, and that had been hours ago, was the ambulance interne's cryptic offer to bet three to one that the wounded girl wouldn't live until they got her on the table.

"Cigarette, Hart?"

"Please?"

Jackson felt a cigarette being inserted between his puffed lips, heard the scratch of a match and inhaled deeply. But no smoke filled his lungs. Instead, an openhanded blow rocked him in his chair.

"Suppose instead of smoking," Lieutenant McCreary of Homicide suggested, "you tell us why you shot Thelma Winston."

"I didn't shoot her."

"Had her shot them."

"I didn't have her shot."

"Don't give us that."

"It's the truth. The Deacon shot her in a try for me."

"By the Deacon you mean Jack Watts?"

"That's right."

"Watts was alone in the car?"

"No. Flip Evans was driving."

Lieutenant McCreary called across the burning circle of light. "You check on Evans yet, Jack?"

"Yeah," an unseen speaker said, "I just got back. Evans swears he didn't leave his apartment all afternoon. And that Watts was right there with him. And both elevator boys and the doorman swear that's so."

Lieutenant McCreary was fair. "Hell! Flip owns the apartment."

"Anyway that's what they said."

McCreary returned his attention to Jackson. "Why not tell the truth, Hart?

It'll make things easier at your trial."

"My trial for what?"

"Murder."

"I haven't killed anyone."

"You'll be charged with it if the girl dies."

Jackson digested the information. The interne had been wrong. Thelma was still alive.

"You've known Thelma for how long?"

"I don't know her. She's new since my time."

"You saw her for the first time at a bus stop outside the prison?"

"Yes."

"And she trailed you back to Chicago and asked you to marry her in a North Clark Street bar?"

"That's the way it happened."

"You think a jury will believe that?"

"It's the truth."

Jackson heard rather than felt the slap. His numbed body refused to feel further pain.

"You lie," Lieutenant McCreary said without emotion. "Now, isn't it true that to get even for your fancied grudge against Evans you've been slipping letters out of Stateville for some time begging Thelma to marry you as soon as you got out?"

"No. It isn't."

"Yet she shows up with a license in her purse less than five hours after you spring free on parole."

"That's the way it was."

"Why did she want to marry you?"

"She didn't say." Jackson remembered. "Yes, she did. I asked her the same question and she said, 'Don't ask me how I know, but you're a right guy, Jackson. The kind of a guy I used to think I'd fall in love with. A man who fights for what he knows is right — a man who takes care of his own.'"

A snigger rippled around the room.

McCreary said dryly, "And that was the start of a beautiful barroom romance." He tried another tack. "Just between the two of us, Hart, how much did you promise the guy who chopped her down for you?"

33

"Nothing."

"You mean he did it for friendship? It was some guy you'd done time with?"

Jackson tried to close his eyes against the pain and a detective standing behind him yanked them open with a vicious tug at his hair. "The lieutenant asked you a question."

"I've told the lieutenant who shot her."

"The hell of it is," McCreary said, "I don't believe you." He brushed Jackson's face with a paper. "Know what this is, Hart?"

"No."

"It's an insurance policy. A policy for ten thousand dollars on Thelma's life — with you named as beneficiary. We found it in the poor kid's purse."

Jackson tried to think. The blonde had mentioned more money, a lot more money, in fact, ten thousand dollars! She'd known or been afraid that she was going to die. But she'd wanted to marry him first because of Olga.

Jackson locked the name in his inner mind. It could be the key to this thing. The police didn't have anything on him, not even a gun. This was just a searching expedition.

"You know about this policy?"

"No."

McCreary restrained his temper with an obvious effort. "Look. Be reasonable, Hart. We don't get any kick knocking you around. It's just our job. Come on. Be a good fellow."

"How?"

"Admit you hired someone to chop Thelma and we'll send out for some sandwiches and coffee."

Jackson felt a lighted cigarette being stuck between his lips. He sucked at it and this time his lungs filled with smoke.

"That's the fellow," McCreary complimented. "I'll send downstairs for a police stenographer and you can dictate your confession."

Jackson shook his head. "I can't"

"You can't what?" McCreary asked.

"Confess. Why should I hire anyone to shoot the kid? I never saw her before this morning."

A hard palm smacked his cheek. The cigarette flew from his lips. The questioning continued.

"Why did you come back to Chicago?"

"To kill Flip Evans."

"You admit that?"

"Yes."

"Why?"

His mind numbed with pain and fatigue, Jackson told the truth. "Because Flip murdered Helene Adele during a drunken brawl and tried to pin it on my kid bother Jerry."

"On your kid brother? I thought you went up for twenty years on that rap."

"I did. When I saw the frame was tight, I got Jerry out of the apartment and took the rap myself."

"Why?"

Hart Jackson had often wondered that himself. The closest to a solution he had ever reached was the realization that at the time Jerry had been a kid and a right guy took care of his own one way or another.

"Why?" McCreary repeated. "And why are you spilling this now?"

Jackson's puffed lips spread in a grotesque smile. "Because it doesn't matter now. He's dead."

"Who's dead?

"Jerry."

"Killed in a heist somewhere?" McCreary sneered.

Jackson shook his head. "No. He was shot down over Vietnam. I got the official cablegram in Stateville yesterday!"

A brief hush filled the smoke-choked room.

"I'm sorry," McCreary said finally. Look. You've been a big shot, Hart. You've made more in two weeks than any guy in the squad room ever made in a year. What's more you're smart. You aren't the kind of a lug we usually have under the light. But you're in a tight spot, fellow. Your story doesn't make sense. And if you talk, well, you'll be making it easier on us all."

Jackson protested, "But how can I talk, McCreary? I've got nothing to say except what I've said. I never saw or heard of Thelma Winston until she walked up to that bus stop this morning."

"You lie," McCreary said heavily.

Jackson closed his eyes. The detective behind him yanked them open. McCreary held a gun in front of his face.

"You do admit though that this unfired .38 is yours?"

Jackson considered the matter. Admitting ownership of the gun would automatically revoke his parole. He knew now why Thelma had yanked it from his pocket. He hadn't had a chance against the Deacon and if he lived through the shooting, the blonde girl hadn't wanted him sent back to Stateville. She wanted him free to watch over the mysterious Olga, whoever she might be.

Jackson lied for the first time. "No. I never saw it before."

One of the detectives in the group around the chair swore softly. "For Chrissakes, let's bust it up. He ain't going to talk an' my knuckles are sore from pounding on the guy."

McCreary slapped Jackson a last time. "Then if the girl dies, your defense is going to be that it was Flip and the Deacon who chopped her?"

"It was."

"I doubt it," McCreary said. "Why should Flip Evans want to kill his own moll?"

The light in front of Jackson's eyes blanked out briefly. He swam back through the dark. "I don't believe it."

"You don't believe what?"

"That Thelma Winston was Flip's girl."

McCreary hooted. "Oh, but she was. Where do you think she got that silver fox fur she was wearing? And the five hundred we found in her purse? And the apartment she lived in?" His tone was slightly envious. "That fat gut makes them all. You ought to know. You were the M.C. at the Club Bali for two years."

The thought of Flip's fat hands fondling

Thelma made Jackson slightly sick to his stomach. Whatever she was, the kid was far too good for Flip. He knew how Flip treated his woman. Jackson cupped is head in his hands. No one tried to stop him. No one slapped him or pulled his hair. Lieutenant McCreary switched off the bright light and turned on the ceiling globe.

"That's all for tonight, boys," McCreary dismissed his squad. "It would seem that Mr. Jackson isn't going to nominate himself on the first ballot. But we'll vote again if we have to to." He delegated one of the detectives. "Take him upstairs, Charlie. The usual. Suspicion of homicide."

Jackson got heavily to his feet. "How's she doing?" he asked McCreary.

"Who?"

"You know who I mean, Thelma."

McCreary shook his head. "Not so hot. The last time I called County they didn't think she'd make it."

"You've talked to her?"

"No."

"Why not?"

McCreary's grin was wry. "Mainly because she can't talk. The doc that I talked to said that even if she does pull through, it may be a week before we can question her."

The detective detailed to take Jackson up to the lockup snapped a handcuff on his wrist. "Let's go fellow."

Jackson continued to hold back. "Just one more thing, McCreary."

"What?"

"If I were you I'd detail a couple of boys to guard her. It could be that I'm not lying to you and it just occurred to me that the Deacon and Flip may not have given a damn about getting me as long as they got Thelma."

Lieutenant McCreary was amused. "And why would they want to get Thelma?"

Jackson watched McCreary's face for reaction as he used the name. "Maybe because of Olga."

Lieutenant McCreary merely looked puzzled. "And who the hell is Olga?"

"I wish I knew." Jackson admitted.

4

IT had been two nights since Thelma had been gone. Olga was lonely. She was frightened. She was so hungry she couldn't sleep.

She studied her reflection in the mirror of the dressing table. She had a pretty body. It was even prettier now that she'd put on a pair of Thelma's sheer hose, a pair of filmy panties and a wisp of a brassiere. She wished the girls in Shelby could see her. Their eyes would pop and then some.

Olga considered her makeup. She thought she looked a trifle pale and added more blusher. It added considerably to her coloring but did nothing for the rumbling in her stomach. Her too-red lips thrust outward in a pout. Thelma had promised to come back by morning. And she still hadn't come.

The girl in front of the mirror tugged

her stockings tighter. It would soon be night or morning. Time always confused her a little. She studied Thelma's diamond wristwatch. It said twenty minutes after seven. No. The other hand was the long one. Olga made a mental calculation. That made it twenty-five minutes of four. Back on the farm, Uncle John would soon be getting up to do his morning chores. If it wasn't for loving Thelma as much as she did, she could wish she was back on the farm. This going without eating was silly.

She raised the drawn blind on the window cautiously and looked out. Underneath the tracks of the elevated electric train on which she and Thelma had ridden, the red neon sign was still outlined boldly against the morning: *TERMINAL RESTAURANT Steaks and Chops.*

Uncle John often ate steak for breakfast along with a big heap of pancakes and a platter of fried eggs. The thought made Olga even hungrier.

She counted the money on the dresser.

There were four, five, six, seven dollars. It wasn't fair for Thelma to leave her so much money and then forbid her to go out and spend it.

Olga considered the matter carefully. She'd eaten in the restaurant in Shelby lots of times. Real meals, too. Not counting Cokes and ice cream cones. She could eat fast and come right back to the room and Thelma wouldn't even know she'd been gone.

She looked out the window again. During the afternoon it had been warm. Now it was beginning to snow. As far as she could see, the parkway was covered with white.

Determined, Olga stood up. As she did the brassiere and panties fell off leaving her completely nude except for the stockings that fitted her like hip boots. Thelma's clothes simply would not fit her. She would have to wear her own. Her own warm underthings, soft woolen dress and heavy coat were piled carefully on the chair. Olga thrust a well-shaped leg into the suit of long woolen underwear. Perhaps when she'd been in the city longer she would fill out more and she could wear Thelma's things.

"I'm hungry and I'm going to eat," she told the mirror as she dressed.

Then she remembered her promise.

Promise, now, sweetheart, Thelma had said, holding her close to her. *Promise you won't leave the room for any reason. Cross your heart and hope to die.*

Cross my heart and hope to die, she had promised. *I won't leave the room until you get back.* And she'd spit on her palm, too, to seal the promise.

Tears coursed between the freckles the rouge couldn't quite hide. She didn't want to break her promise to Thelma. She didn't want to die. But she was so hungry — so awfully hungry.

It was then she had the idea. Olga didn't know why she hadn't thought of it before. The phone number was easy to find. It was printed on the blow-out thing that made noise that she'd packed up in the sort-of-like-a-restaurant-only-different-place where Thelma sang pretty songs.

Olga tried to pronounce the name. It was Club Belly, or something like that the number was easier. It was Shore, like on the lake than a six and four ones. She picked up the phone and told the operator the number.

"Club Bali," a man's voice said crisply as the connection was completed.

"If you please," Olga said distinctly into the mouthpiece as Aunt Sonia had taught her, "I would like to speak to Thelma."

There was a brief pause at the other end. Then a man's voice said. "Why — sure. Just a moment, please. I'll call her to the phone."

Olga had never been so pleased with Olga until the second voice answered. It wasn't Thelma's voice at all. It was the voice of the fat man who had made the gray-haired man's face all bloody.

"Say, I'm awfully sorry. Thelma is busy right now," he apologized pleasantly. "But she asked me to take the message. Who is this calling? And what is it you want me to tell her?"

"This is Olga, her sister," Olga told him. "And tell Thelma to please come home," She tried not to cry and failed. "Tell her I'm hungry and lonesome."

The fat man continued to be pleasant. "Sure thing, honey. I'll see she comes home right away. But — er — where are you calling from?"

"Why — " Olga began and stopped speaking. She didn't know exactly why, but she knew that Thelma would not be pleased if she told the man where she was. That was why Thelma had left the pretty apartment and come to this hotel — so no one would know where they were.

The fat man was shouting into the phone now. "Answer me. You hear me? Where are you? Where are you calling from?"

A moment of silence followed then another man's voice said, "You couldn't get the address, huh?"

The fat man was very angry. He said a bad word. "No. The little bitch hung up."

Olga realized she was still holding the receiver and put it back on the hook. Tears flooded her eyes. Her slim shoulders shook. She threw herself on the bed and sobbed.

She was lonely. She was hungry. She was frightened. Even playing grownup lady in Thelma's clothes and using her rouge and lipstick had lost all of its magic. She was after all, only seven. And until Aunt Sonia had died and Uncle John had sent her to live with Thelma, she had never been in a city before ...

The lights had been dimmed for the night. Only one low watt bulb burned in the ceiling. A thought amused Jackson. Seven long years ago he wouldn't have had the least idea what lay between him and freedom. Now he was well acquainted with penal routine from the county jail up.

At the end of the short corridor

there should be an unarmed turnkey, his chair tipped back against the wall, nodding over the midnight edition of the morning paper. Beyond him, there should be a desk screw, working on the nightbook work, bringing the records up to date. Beyond the desk screw through still another bolted door lay the bank of elevators that he must somehow reach. Whatever he did, he would have to be fairly clever. A forced crushout was out of the question. Such things just didn't happen.

The night's business had been dull, at least in the upper brackets. The drunk tanks might be filled but he and an old-lag con man were the only customers in the detention block assigned to homicide.

"Cigarette?" Jackson asked the man.

The man in the next cell extended an arm through the front bars of his cell until his groping fingers made contact with the package. "Thanks. Thanks a lot, fellow."

"Keep the pack," Jackson told him. "I'm going out."

49

The old lag laughed."You're nuts. You're eleven floors above the street. And even if you could get out of your cell, you got the turnkey, the desk screw and the elevator guard to dodge."

"Now you tell me," Jackson said. He gripped the bars of his cell and called to the dozing guard. "Hey! Turnkey! Be a pal, will you? Move me into another cell. This one is lousy with rats."

The turnkey lowered the front legs of his chair to the floor. "G'wan to sleep, Jackson. You're seein' things. We ain't got no rats up here."

"No? Keep quiet and listen."

Jackson gripped his cell, still staring full-faced at the turnkey. Apparently from the darkened corner of the cell behind him, a rat squealed viciously. It was joined by a second and third.

The turnkey said, "I'll be damned."

The old lag laughed. "They must be holding a conversation."

"Be a pal," Jackson repeated. "All I ask is that you move me to another cell."

The turnkey waddled down the corridor and peered past Jackson into the cell. The squealing under the bunk resumed. The turnkey repeated that he would be damned, inserted the key in the lock and swung the cell door open.

"We used to have plenty of rats out at County," he told Jackson, "But these are the first I ever saw up here. Must have come through the drain, eh?"

"Could be," Jackson said.

The turnkey bent to peer under the bunk and Jackson hit him back of the ear with a balled fist and caught him as he fell.

"You're clever, pal," the con man complimented. "You ought to be on the stage."

"I was," Jackson told him.

He bound and gagged the unconscious man with strips torn from the blanket. Then putting on his hat and overcoat he stepped out of the cell, locking it behind him.

"You want out?" he asked the old lag. The con man shook his head. "Uh uh. They got nothing on me I can't beat. Besides, you aren't going to make it, pal."

"Could be" Jackson admitted.

He stood a moment with his back pressed to the bars of the cell he had just quitted. It could be he was being foolish. As with the man in the cell, McCreary had nothing on him he couldn't beat providing Thelma lived. But would she? McCreary didn't believe his story. And having made one try for the girl, Flip Evans might well make another.

Then there was Olga.

"Lose your nerve?" the old lag asked.

"No," Jackson said. "Just thinking."

He walked to the far end of the corridor and flattened himself against the wall beside the door. His voice, the fat turnkey's voice now, rose in excitement as he beat on the steel door with one fist. "Hey, Jim. Come in here a minute, will ya? I think that guy Jackson that McCreary just brought in is trying to do a Dutch."

On the far side of the door a chair

scraped heavily on concrete. "How?"

"With strips cut from his blanket."

"Well, cut him down, you damn fool!" the desk screw shouted. A key turned in the lock. Steel rasped on steel. "There'll be hell to pay if — "

Jackson swung the turnkey's sap as the desk screw came through the door.

"Boy," the old lag enthused, "You're good. The guy never knew what hit him."

Jackson transferred the unconscious officer's gun from its holster to his own pocket. Then he removed his shield and pinned it to the inside of his coat lapel and closed and bolted the door of steel.

His envelope was still on the screw's desk. Jackson took the roll of bills from it and opened the hall door. Jackson turned up the collar of his coat as if against the expected outside cold and called back into the booking office. "You want that Swiss on whole wheat or rye, Jim?"

"On rye," the desk screw's voice called

back. "And don't forget to stop in the D.A.'s office and see if you can get the file on that guy McCreary just brought in."

Detectives came. Detectives went. Catching the exposed flash of silver, the hall guard yawned and resumed his pacing as Jackson punched the elevator button boldly.

The cage operator was old. He looked at Jackson without interest and reversed his lever. "It's turned cold," he offered.

Jackson controlled his breathing with an effort, "So?"

"Yeah," the old man nodded. "Snowing too. I knew damn well that nice weather wouldn't last."

He made stops at the eighth and fifth and fourth floors. None of them paid any attention to Jackson. McCreary and his squad had gone off duty.

As he crossed the slush streaked foyer to the street, Jackson turned the collar of his coat still higher. His legs were beginning to tremble. His shoes squished as he walked. No one recognized him.

No one called after him. No one tried to stop him.

The night was black. The wind felt cold on his sweat-drenched body. Except for several official cars, one lone cab parked at the curb, an occasional weary officer walking head down against the wind and the lights in the Coffee Pot on the far side of the parking lot, lower South State Street was deserted.

Jackson stood in front of the building briefly, flipping a mental coin. There were three things he wanted to do before he was picked up again. He wanted to make certain that Thelma was safe. He wanted to talk to Olga. He wanted to beat in Flip Evan's teeth, do what he'd returned to Chicago to do.

He decided to talk to Olga first and crossed the deserted walk to the parked cab. The flag was up. Jackson opened the door of the cab.

"The Logan — " he began and stopped.

The flag of the cab was up but the back seat was occupied. Two cigarette tips glowed in the dark. One hand reaching for the gun he'd taken from the desk screw, Jackson started to back out.

"Uh uh," Deacon Watts warned him. "I've got a gun in my hand. And it's been leveled at your belly since you walked out that door." His voice was incredulous. "How the hell did you get out?"

"Walked out," Jackson said dully.

Watt's voice was still incredulous. "Boy! Talk about breaks of the game. Here me and the best mouthpiece in Chicago sit freezing to death figuring how to spring you. We decide it can't be done — and you drop right into our laps."

Jackson stiffened his body against the expected shot. It didn't come.

"Get in," Watts ordered. He moved over to make room for Jackson then changed his mind. "No. Get in front with Sam."

"Where to, Deacon?" the driver asked.

The vicious little gunman chuckled.

"Let's go to the Club." He pressed the barrel of the gun in his hand to the back of Jackson's head. "Flip thinks that Pretty Boy, here, might know where Olga is."

5

AS he ate his belated supper, McCreary watched great flaky crystals of snow pelt the kitchen window and was pleased.

"Bunny will like that," he told his wife. "She can use her sled in the morning. If it snows enough, I'll take her over to the park, huh?"

Betty McCreary cut another slice of beef from the shrunken roast that had been ready to serve at one o'clock. "That will be nice. But how come you're so late dear?"

McCreary considered the question. A man of little imagination, he left the day's work behind him as soon as he signed out. Tonight somehow, it was different. What if Jackson hadn't been lying? What if he had been telling the truth?

"On account of we had to sweat a guy

named Hart Jackson," he told her.

"Who did he kill?"

McCreary shook his head. "The girl isn't dead yet. At least, she wasn't dead the last time I called County." He had to have outside advice. "But look, hon — "

"Yes — ?"

McCreary started to tell her the story and didn't know where to begin. The longer he thought about it, the less sense Jackson's story made. No smart man in his sane mind would attempt to sell such a story to a squad of hard-boiled homicide men unless it were true and he had no other story to tell.

Betty McCreary mulled the name. "Hart Jackson? Wasn't that the name of that clever ventriloquist we saw at the Chez Paree? You know, the time we blew ourselves. On our fifth anniversary. The one who looks something like Tony Curtis."

"That's the guy."

"But I thought he was in prison."

"He got out on parole this morning."

"And he's in trouble again?"

"Yeah."

"What did he do?"

"We think he killed this girl or had her killed."

"Why?"

"The way I see it, to get even with Flip Evans. He claims now that Flip framed him on that Helene Adele rap. That is, he claims Flip framed his brother and he took the rap. His kid brother, see?"

"Oh. And where is his brother now?"

"Shot down over Vietnam, Jackson says." McCreary suddenly wasn't hungry. He pushed his plate away. "Look. Here's the story he tells us, hon — "

"Yes — ?"

"He says this blonde who got shot came down to Joliet this morning and asked him to marry her. Out of a clear sky, see?"

"She'd known him before?"

"He says not. He says he never saw her until she showed up this morning."

"Then why did she want to marry him?"

"That's what struck him. The only thing he could come up with was he asked her the same question and she said he was a right guy who took care of his own."

"Then she knew he'd been framed, that he'd taken the rap for his brother?"

McCreary hadn't thought of that angle. He filed it away for further reference. "Could be."

"This girl who was shot was pretty?"

"Very. She was also Evans' girl. We've established that."

"And Jackson married her?"

"About four-thirty this afternoon."

"What happened then?"

"According to his story, they're standing in front of the minister's who married them when Flip Evans and a hood named Watts drive up and Watts empties an automatic. Jacksons claims first they were shooting at him then he changes his story and say he thinks they were after the girl."

"You arrested this Evans and this Watts?"

61

McCreary shook his head. "Uh uh. They're big stuff, see? Evans owns the Club Bali and plenty of other stuff in town."

"So you let them go and beat on Jackson."

"No. Not exactly. I had Jack check on them. And he brought back a clean bill of goods. According to what he could gather, neither Evans nor Watts had been out of Evans' apartment." McCreary continued to massage his skinned knuckles. "On the other hand, Evans owns the building. And while no one else sees the car Jackson claims they were in, Evans is the kind of a fat bastard who'd gun his own grandmother for the silk ribbons in her prayer book."

"Then why not take Jackson's word?"

McCreary pushed back his chair and stood up. "I'll tell you why. Because his story is screwball. Because no pretty dame like the one who was shot, at least no dame who would play house with a louse like Flip Evans for what she could get out of him, is going to ask a penniless ex-con to marry her just because he's a right guy. It don't hold up, see? Besides, we find this insurance policy in her purse. A policy for ten grand with Jackson named as beneficiary."

"That doesn't prove he killed her or had her killed."

McCreary gripped the back of his chair. "No."

Betty McCreary got up and stood beside her husband. "What's worrying you, John?"

McCreary told her. "I'd like to believe the guy, see? That's why I pound on him so hard tonight. For two reasons. One, I think Jackson's a pretty good Joe."

"And two?"

McCreary exhaled the breath he'd been holding. "I'd like to get Evans, see? The whole department would. For ten years now on account of his political pull, we have to go around saying yes, sir and no, sir, shutting our eyes to things we'd slam other guys in the can for so fast it would make their heads swim. But when we do get him, we've got to get him right."

"I see."

McCreary cursed softly under his breath as the phone in the bedroom tinkled. "Oh, my God! Now what?"

He padded down the short hall in his stockinged feet. The bedroom was warm and smelled of sleep. "That you, Daddy?" a small sleepy voice asked from the darkness.

McCreary ignored the ringing phone to sit on the edge of the bed. "Look, Bunny. You're supposed to be asleep," he told his daughter.

He bent and kissed her hot little forehead. "And you'd better sleep real fast and get good and rested."

"Why?" the small voice asked.

"Because it's snowing. And you and me are going sledding in the morning."

The seven-year-old snuggled into a sleepy ball. "That's super."

Lieutenant McCreary reached through the dark for the phone. "McCreary speaking."

His wife watched him with worried eyes as he returned to the kitchen, forced his swollen feet into his shoes and buckled on his shoulder holster.

"Now what, John?" she asked.

McCreary reached for his coat. "Well, that would seem to take care of that."

"Take care of what?"

"Whether or not Jackson killed the girl."

"What's happened now?"

McCreary shaped his wet hat to his head. "He just busted out of Central Bureau. From the eleventh floor, mind you. And he damn near killed a turnkey busting out!"

After the cold of the street it was hot inside the cab. It smelled of good tobacco and, more faintly, of good whiskey. From the back seat Attorney Diamond said, "If there's going to be any rough stuff, let me out when we get to the Loop."

The Deacon laughed. "There's not going to be any rough stuff, Counselor. We're just going to beat Hart's brains in, that's all. Unless he plays it smart and tells us where Olga is."

Jackson rode looking at the falling snow, conscious of the gun barrel nuzzling the nape of his neck. If he tried to make a break, the Deacon wouldn't hesitate; he'd pull the trigger of the gun.

It wasn't fair that out of all the taxicabs in Chicago, he'd had to pick the one in which Jack Watts and Max Diamond were sitting. Still it hadn't been coincidence. Watts, better known to the habitués of the Club Bali as the Deacon because of his poker face and somber manner of dress, had crowed:

Boy! Talk about breaks of the game. Here me and the best mouthpiece in Chicago sit freezing to death, figuring how to spring you. We decide it can't be done — and you drop right into our laps.

No. It hadn't been coincidence. They had been sitting in front of the Bureau trying to figure some way to spring him. Why? Because they thought he knew where Olga was. Because for some reason, Olga, whoever she was, was important to Flip Evans.

As the cab turned east toward the Outer Drive, Diamond said, "You're joking, of course?"

"About what?" Watts asked.

"Beating in Jackson's brains unless he talks."

Hart could sense the Deacon moving his head from side to side as he grunted, "Uh uh. Unless he opens up and tells us where Olga is, he's going to get it — but good."

Diamond sounded worried. "Then let me out. Anywhere along here will do. I'll pick up another taxi."

"Uh, uh," the Deacon repeated. "You saw him get into the cab. And if anything should go sour, you might turn chicken and talk. Besides, you've taken Flip's money and it could be we'll need you."

The lawyer began another protest, realized the futility of it and lapsed into an uneasy silence.

The incident, Jackson thought, was symbolic of the way Flip Evans operated. You took the fat man's money for one thing and the next thing you knew you found yourself up to the neck in one of his nefarious schemes. It had been that way with Jerry. Not that it mattered now. His kid brother was dead, a name in the last statistic issued by the War Department.

The gun barrel slapped the back of Hart's head lightly. "How'd you do it, fellow?" the Deacon asked. "We gave you credit for being smart but not smart enough to bust out of the Bureau."

Jackson told him the truth. "I talked my way out."

"I'll bet you."

Jackson started to reply, then turned his head sharply as the wail of a police siren filled the cab.

The cab driver tossed a quick glance over his shoulder. "Jeez. Now what, Deacon?"

The Deacon was unperturbed. "Keep right on going."

"But I hear a police car."

"Sure. Hart's doing it with his mouth. It used to be part of his act when he was M.C. at the Club. Whenever one of the strippers peeled down to the promised land and then reached for her G-string, Hart used to make like the cops were raiding the joint." The Deacon added, "All of us used to damn near die laughing watching the cheaters scramble to get out on account of they thought the joint was pinched."

The strident wail of the siren cut out as abruptly as it had begun. "You've got a good memory, Jack," Hart said. "But who is this Olga? Why is she so important? Why all the fuss about her?"

"As if you didn't know."

"I don't"

The gun barrel slapped the back of Hart's head again, not so lightly this time. "Don't give me that. Thelma told you all about it on the way from Stateville." There was begrudging admiration in the Deacon's voice. "Now there is one little broad who is as smart as she is pretty. Here we are combing the town for her and Olga. And what does Thelma do? She plays it smart. She drives down to Stateville and offers to crawl in bed with the one guy with a grudge against Flip who's got the guts to try to do something about it. A lusty guy who hasn't had a woman for seven years. And all he has to do in exchange for her fair white body is get her and Olga out of Chicago. Where were you figuring on taking her, Hart? Back to the farm where she came from?"

The cab driver asked, "This Thelma, the kid that got shot, is that the well-stacked little blonde who crooned the torch songs on the Rounders' Lullaby?"

"That's the one. We were lucky one of the boys spotted her down at the bus station." The Deacon was amused. "A shame you didn't get to consummate your marriage, Hart. I hear that Thelma is a hot little number."

Hart wanted to turn and beat at the smirk on the other man's face. He couldn't see it but he knew it was there. He wished now he'd listened to Thelma in the bus station at Joliet. He wished he'd insisted she tell him the whole story before he'd married her. But right up to

70

the final 'I do' he'd thought the whole thing was a gag. He hadn't realized she was serious, that she had meant to be his wife. He'd thought she was just acting as a lure for Flip Evans.

Hart managed to keep his voice casual. "How is she doing, Jack?"

The Deacon was even more amused. "Not so good the last time I hear. The police are afraid she'll die before she can put the finger on you. Not that it makes any difference to you. As soon as you tell us where Olga is, you're leaving town again. Permanently this time."

"For God's sake," Diamond said. "Don't even talk like that. Not while I'm in the cab."

"See?" the Deacon jeered. "It's a good thing I didn't let you out when you wanted out. Nothing has happened so far and you're turning chicken already."

Hart asked, "And what happens if I don't know where Olga is?"

The Deacon was matter-of-fact about it. "That would be very bad. For you. Because we know better, see? You aren't

71

dealing with a punk, Hart. Flip was big time before he had you tucked away. And he's even bigger time now. And the first thing Thelma would tell you would be where she had stashed Olga."

That much was true, Jackson thought. But it hadn't been the first but the last thing that Thelma had told him. He closed his eyes and saw her lying on the muddy grass between the sidewalk and the curb, blood staining her white blouse.

I meant to, Hart she had whispered. *And I didn't mean this to happen. I didn't know I'd been followed.* Then she'd told him it was up to him to take care of Olga. *She's at the Logan Square Hotel. In Room 410.*

The Deacon asked, "By the way, where is she?"

"I don't know," Jackson lied. "I haven't the least idea."

The man in the back seat of the cab swung the gun barrel in a short but vicious arc. "There's a small memory pill to help refresh your mind. And

72

you'd better know by the time we get to the Club. Because I'm going to enjoy working on you. I always did hate a slob who thought he was better than I am."

Sick with the pain of the blow, Hart leaned against the rolled up window. The cold glass felt good against his hot cheek. He couldn't take another beating, not after the one he'd just had. And this one would be different. Neither Flip nor the Deacon would stop at anything. They'd use every dirty trick in the book. They'd torture him and beat on him until he couldn't take any more. Then he'd tell them where Olga was.

The hell I will, he thought.

The little blonde had made a bargain with him, even if she had never gotten a chance to explain it. When he had asked her why she wanted to marry him, she'd told him: *Don't ask me how I know, but you're a right guy, Jackson. The kind of a guy I used to think I'd fall in love with. A man who fights for what he knows is right — a man who takes care of his own.* More, she had meant to keep her bargain. She'd been willing to check into a hotel, any hotel, with him as Mrs. Hart Jackson. Now if she was still alive, she was fighting for her life. He couldn't let her down. He wouldn't.

Jackson straightened in the seat and the Deacon asked with mock solicitude, "You feel a little queasy, huh?"

"A little," Jackson admitted.

When the pain had cleared sufficiently for him to see, he rode staring through the snow-flecked windshield, listening to the snick of the wipers, waiting for a break in the stream of oncoming headlights. If possible in doing what he planned to do, Jackson didn't want any innocent bystanders to be hurt.

The Deacon said, soberly. "The hell of it is, fellow, unless you smart up fast, you're going to feel a lot worse before you feel better."

The speeding cab was less than five blocks from the Club Bali now. Jackson doubted he'd leave the Club alive. The Deacon would see to that. Once he and Flip Evans had learned what they wanted to know, they would be foolish to turn him loose again. There was always a chance that Lieutenant McCreary might believe his story.

Glancing up at the rear vision mirror, Jackson saw the poker-faced gunman start to swing the gun barrel again, in a much wider arc this time. Jackson slid down in the seat and the barrel of the gun thudded against the metal frame of the pushed-back glass partition.

The Deacon cursed him without heat.

Jackson then thrust his left leg across the driver's ankle, stomped hard on the brake and yanked at the wheel of the speeding cab.

As the cab skidded across the Drive, the driver fought Jackson for the wheel screaming, "Knock him out! For God's sake, knock him out! The guy is nuts."

The Deacon thrust his head and shoulders through the opening between the front and back seats and beat at Jackson with his gun. "Cut it out, you damn fool! You'll kill us all."

Evading the gun as best he could,

Jackson kicked the driver's feet away, shoved up on the wheel and pressed the accelerator to the floor boards.

The cab spun in a full circle, then skidded back across the snow covered pavement into the stream of southbound traffic. There was a blare of horns and a squealing of brakes as two southbound cars barely avoided being struck by the metal juggernaut. The cab skidded into the curb, blowing the two left tires. Then as Jackson stomped on the gas again, it made a full revolution before skidding sideways into a stout metal light pole rising out of a heavy cement safety island.

There was a screech of tortured metal, then the cab came to a stop on its side with the lamp post on top of it.

6

JACKSON'S mouth felt like it was filled with blood. The driver's body was an inert mass under his knees. Somewhere in the back of the cab, the Deacon was cursing softly as if he were in pain. Diamond was either unconscious or dead.

Jackson tried to put his weight on the wheel and there was none. All that was left was the post. The steering wheel had broken off in the driver's hands. He felt through the dark for the handle of the door and pushed up on it. The door was jammed. He tried again and heard voices as other motorists stopped their cars and got out to help.

Several of them climbed on the cab and forced the door open. Jackson climbed out slowly with the aid of the two men who had forced the door.

"How many others in there, buddy?"

one of the men asked him.

"Three," Jackson told him. "The driver and two fares in back."

The other man asked, "What happened? The driver drunk or what? He damn near skidded into me."

"I think he was drunk," Jackson said.

He climbed slowly off the cab as one of the two men standing on it yelled for someone to hand him a flashlight. A crowd had collected swiftly and traffic was already blocked for half a block in both directions.

Jackson flexed his fingers then his arms. His fingers moved. He could walk. He did not hurt anywhere. Nothing seemed to be broken. He stood a moment watching the two men, aided by three other men now, light the interior of the cab with borrowed flashlights.

One of the men on the cab said, "I think the driver and one of the guys in back are dead. But the other guy is holding his arm as if it's broken."

As he finished speaking the Deacon screamed, "Get me out of here! Goddam it! Don't just stand there looking at me! Get me out of here!"

As a dozen men surged forward, Jackson moved back through the falling snow into the ranks of the curious newcomers.

"What happened?" one of them asked him.

Jackson said, "A cab skidded out of control."

A police car was coming now. He could see its revolving red light less than a block away. Jackson walked slowly out of the fast-forming crowd and west on Ohio Street. So Diamond and the driver were dead. He felt no sense of guilt. All he felt was great relief. He'd gambled his life and won. It wasn't his fault if the cab driver and the lawyer had crapped out.

There was something binding his forehead. Jackson put one hand to his head and realized his hat was crammed down over his ears. It was the leather sweat band that was binding him. He tugged his hat loose and walked on, shaping it as he walked, the wet snow felt good on his face.

Back at the scene of the accident, other sirens were wailing now. Jackson was grimly amused. For once in his life the Deacon was in a spot. He wouldn't dare say who had been the fourth man in the cab. If he did the police would charge him with being an accessory to an escape.

There were few cars and no pedestrians on the street. Jackson looked at his wrist automatically and remembered he'd pawned his watch. When? So much had happened. Morning seemed years ago. He'd pawned his watch to buy a gun. And the police had the gun now. If he ever got to Flip Evans he'd have to kill him with his hands. But first there was Olga to consider.

Jackson walked a little faster. Michigan Boulevard was wider and brighter than the side street. He crossed it and continued west on Ohio towards Clark Street. There was a bar on the corner of Clark Street. The Venetian blinds were drawn but both light and music seeped out the partly opened door.

Jackson pushed the door and walked in. The smoke in the place was so thick it made breathing difficult. Despite the lateness of the hour all the booths were occupied. So were the bar stools. On a raised platform back of the bar, a pretty brunette barely out of her teens was doing a listless strip tease.

Jackson pushed up to the bar. "A double rye and a beer," he told the man back of the wood. "Make it Old Overholt and let's see the bottle when you pour it."

The barman wasn't insulted. "You're the doctor, fellow. Been pitching a bit of a wing-ding, huh?"

Jackson felt his face. His left eye was puffed. In a few minutes it would be swollen shut. His smile was tight. "A small one."

The rye tasted good. He washed it down with the beer and walked back to the washroom just as the teaser on the platform finished her act to a smattering of applause.

The sound nauseated Jackson. He'd worked in plenty of such places before he'd become *the* Hart Jackson. But that had been a long time ago. If the bluenoses and reformers who were always trying to clean up such places would bring back vaudeville and burlesque, maybe cute kids like the little brunette stripper could break into show business without having to sing dirty songs or take off all their clothes.

The washroom attendant ran water in a bowl and laid out a towel and comb. Jackson washed his face and combed his hair. His left eye was going to be a beauty. But outside of the eye and a small cut inside his mouth, he'd come out all right. He tipped the attendant a half dollar and walked back to the bar.

"Let's try it again," he told the barman.

Another little stripper, a blonde girl this time, was beginning her tease by taking off a wide-brimmed picture hat and reaching for the zipper of her dress. Her voice was sweet and clear, but none of the drunks at the bar were interested in her voice. She reminded Jackson of Thelma. The cab driver had called her a singer — *that well-stacked little blonde who crooned the torch songs on the Rounders' Lullaby.*

Still, a barman down the street had known her. He had called her by name, Miss Winston. It was possible, very possible, that Thelma had stripped on North Clark Street before she had graduated to the Club Bali. If one could call it graduating. The only real difference between the joints on Clark Street and the Club Bali was that at the Club Bali the drinks cost three times as much.

Jackson's feeling of nausea returned. Then he realized what it was. He was jealous. He was in love with his wife, a little blonde he'd never seen until that morning. This was their wedding night and she was dead or dying in County Hospital. Every cop in Chicago was looking for him.

As he gulped his second drink, a teenage B girl pushed her way in between him and the occupied stool on his left. "Lonely, honey?" she asked.

Jackson nodded. "Yeah." He was.

The girl moved closer. "Isn't that funny? So am I." She looked at the change from the ten dollar bill lying on the wood in front of him and ran a pink tongue across her lips. "Want to do something about it? I get through work in half an hour. And I'm awfully good company, honest I am, mister."

The way she said it, she should have had her pretty little mouth washed with soap. Still Jackson was tempted. He'd been in prison for seven years. If he gave the girl a twenty dollar bill, she'd check into some flea bag with him. It would be days before the police could check every hotel in the city. The girl would stay with him as long as his money held out. They could laugh and have fun.

There was another smattering of applause. Jackson looked at the blonde strip teaser. She had completed her act and was standing perfectly nude except for a jeweled G-string and a smile. Her smile was slightly embarrassed. Jackson was embarrassed for her.

The B girl brushed against him. "How about it, honey?"

Jackson pushed his change in front of her. "I'm sorry, kid. No dice. I just got married this afternoon. And my wife's very jealous, I hope."

He walked through the thick blue smoke and babble of drunken voices to the door. The crisp early morning air felt clean.

Despite the fact it was early morning, there were more people on North Clark Street than there had been on Michigan Boulevard and South State and Ohio Streets combined; drunks and would-be wolves and slummers, queers and lesbians and tarts, conventionaires and musicians and actors and just plain lonely men. Virtue, Jackson thought wryly, was still its own reward. North Clark Street hadn't changed in the years he'd been away. Its motto was still the same: If you don't see what you want, ask for it. If you can afford to pay for it, we've got it.

He walked slowly south through the falling snow toward the Loop and climbed the stairs to the long elevated platform on Lake Street. He was anxious to get to Olga. He wished he could take a cab. But cab drivers kept a record of the destination of their trips.

There was a pay phone in the overheated station. Jackson used the classified book and looked up hotels. There was only one Logan Square Hotel on Kedzie Boulevard. As he paid his fare, he asked the old man in the ticket booth what train he took to get to Logan Square and when the next train was due.

"A Logan Square local," the ticket seller told him. "Take the first car. The second car cuts out at Damen and goes out the Humboldt Park spur." He glanced at the clock behind him. "And the next train is due to leave here in four and one-half minutes."

"Thank you," Jackson said.

He bought a handful of quarter cigars

and a paper and walked out onto the snow and wind swept platform. It was like being in another world. Above him the tall buildings of the Loop rose sheer on both sides to disappear into the snow-flecked sky. On the streets below, police cars were tomcatting through the night now, wailing to each other, looking for him, shining their big red eyes into every possible place in which a man might hide. It wasn't a good feeling. The whiskey glow in Jackson's stomach faded. He was glad when the El train came.

There were few people in either car; a loudly snoring drunk, two-red-faced charwomen, a workman well bundled up against the cold and dozing in his seat.

Jackson felt somehow naked and exposed. He expected an officer to board the train at every station at which it stopped. He should have taken a cab. Too much had happened too fast. He wasn't thinking clearly. He could have given the driver some address near the hotel and walked the rest of the distance.

He sat mouthing an unlighted cigar, the paper raised to hide his face.

His escape from Central Bureau and the 'accident' on the Outer Drive weren't as yet headlines. Not enough time had elapsed. They would be in the next edition. There was, however, a good picture of him on the front page. It was one of the glossy prints of him in full evening dress, holding his dummy on his knee. He'd had it taken when he had played the Chez Paree. How long ago? A hundred years. Back in the days when he had hoped he might be a second Edgar Bergen, before he'd gotten tied in with Flip Evans, before the Jerry-Flip-Helene Adele affair, before the seven wasted years during which he had exchanged his name for a number.

Jackson skimmed through the story in the paper then read it, fascinated. He'd never realized a theory so palpably false could sound so logical. The reporter covering the story had already tried and convicted him of the attempted murder of Thelma Winston.

The reporter had even established a motive, of sorts. Jackson had admitted he hated Flip Evans. Thelma was Flip Evans' girl. It said so in black and white. The reporter assumed, just like Lieutenant McCreary had, that he had made love to the girl by mail in letters smuggled out of Stateville. To lull any latent suspicion Thelma might have concerning his motive, he had, according to the reporter, insisted on marrying her within eight hours after he had been released from prison. As he and Thelma had left the parsonage, his hired gunman, as yet unnamed, had been waiting. He had hoped to get even with Flip Evans by blaming the murder on the nightclub owner. But the one mistake that trips nine out of ten murderers had tripped him. In his greed for a stake and perhaps for funds with which to pay his hired gunmen, he had insisted that Thelma insure her life in his favor for ten thousand dollars. The policy had been found in her purse. If the girl died, as it appeared she was going to do, the reporter was certain that the insurance policy along with other evidence he neglected to name would be sufficient to send Hart Jackson back to prison. And this time there would be no nonsense about a parole after he had served seven years. This time the twice-convicted lady killer would go to the electric chair.

"Well, I'll be a son-of-a-bitch," Jackson swore.

One of the charwomen looked up sharply.

Jackson hadn't realized he'd spoken aloud. The last thing he wanted was to attract attention to himself. "I'm sorry," he apologized.

He was relieved when the front door of the car opened and the guard called, "Damen Street. Robey Junction. Car behind for Humboldt Park."

The two women changed to the car behind. The drunk continued to snore. Jackson stared out the window into the storm-filled night. Then as the car got under way again he raised the paper to hide his face as the car flashed past the lighted platform.

To kill time Jackson read the follow-up of the story headlined in the afternoon paper he had been reading in the North Clark Street bar when Thelma had walked in on him with her astounding proposal.

. . . Attorney John M. Masters, representing the Pierce family, expressed grave concern this evening over the continued absence of Fillmore Pierce, noted Loophound and elderly playboy.

Pierce, heir to the Pierce packing-house millions, has not been seen since leaving a popular near-Northside nightclub with an unidentified blonde sometime during the early hours of Thursday morning. Noted for his many eccentricities, however, it is believed that the much-married playboy, accompanied by his pretty companion, may have boarded a plane or train for . . .

Jackson lowered the paper to his lap and rode looking out at the night. He didn't give a damn what had happened to the old goat. He had troubles enough of his own without worrying about the peccadillos of an oversexed wealthy moron.

He rode wondering if both Attorney Diamond and the cab driver were dead. Not that he cared. Both men had asked for what they'd gotten. Then Jackson thought of two words he had spoken and despite the comparatively cool air in the car, he began to sweat. When he had started to get into the cab in front of Central Bureau, he had automatically announced his destination, at least, partially. He had said, "The Logan — " before he realized the cab was occupied. There was only one Logan Square Hotel in the phone book. The Deacon was still alive, very much alive and the Deacon was no fool. If he was Flip Evans wasn't. The chances were that by now the Deacon or another of Flip's boys was racing toward the hotel.

The El train seemed to crawl. Jackson tried to urge it on faster with his body. He was sorry he'd stopped for a drink. He should have gone directly to the hotel.

Now that he knew that Thelma had been Flip's girl, a picture of Olga was beginning to form in his mind. It could be that Olga was Thelma's sister. He pictured a girl slightly younger than his wife, dewy-eyed, innocent, perhaps a farm girl. She had come to visit Thelma and the jaded nightclub owner, tired of Thelma, as he had tired of Helene Adele, as he had tired of countless girls, had made a play for Olga and Thelma had spirited her away.

Jackson took his sodden cigar from his lips and replaced it with a fresh one. Still that didn't add up. There was no reason there for Thelma to want to marry him. And Flip seldom made a fool of himself about any girl. He didn't have to. As Lieutenant McCreary had said: *That fat gut gets them all.*

The whole thing didn't make sense. Why had Thelma wanted to marry him? Why had she insured her life for ten thousand dollars in favor of a perfect stranger? Why had Flip and the Deacon tried to kill her? Why was Olga so important to them? Jackson kneaded his aching temples with the fingers of one hand. He wished he was either smarter or clairvoyant. He wished he could talk to Thelma for just five minutes.

The El car jerked to a sudden halt. "Logan Square, the end of the line," the guard announced.

7

THE snowflakes were smaller now and hard and gritty. There was a new bite to the air. Jackson started across the white square then turned back and looked at the lighted restaurant under the elevated structure. If Olga had been holed up in the hotel since Thelma had started for Stateville, it could be the girl was hungry.

He walked back to the restaurant. "Some sandwiches to go," he told the girl back of the counter. "Whatever you can make up the fastest. A big piece of chocolate cake and about a quart of coffee in a cardboard container."

"Right," the girl nodded. She turned her head and called: "Two ham, two sliced chicken to go. Make 'em on white, in a hurry." The girl looked back at Jackson. "Cream and sugar in the coffee?"

95

"There you have me," Jackson said. "Better put the sugar in a sack and give me a pint of cream."

"You're the doctor," the girl smiled. She filled the two containers and put them in a brown paper sack along with a handful of individual servings of sugar. Then she cut a huge slice of the chocolate cake and wrapped it in wax paper. By the time she had finished, the sandwiches were ready. She sacked them with the coffee and Jackson paid the check and walked back into the night.

It all went to prove something. Perhaps how unobservant people were. There was a morning paper on the counter. The waitress had been reading it when he'd entered the restaurant. His picture was on the front page. It was an excellent likeness. Still she hadn't recognized him. Killers were people in a newspaper or perhaps a true crime magazine, not someone who walked into a restaurant at four o'clock in the morning.

The hotel was small but ultra-modern. A youthful clerk was reading a magazine back of the room desk. Jackson walked in shaking snow from his hat and trying to brush it from his coat.

The youthful clerk was amused. "Some night, eh, sir? Especially after that touch of spring we had."

Jackson set the paper sack down on the counter. "Some night is right," he agreed. "I pay a little social call and now I can't even get my car started. How are the chances of getting a room?"

The clerk laid a registration card on the counter. "Fine. With or without?"

"Without will do," Jackson said. He signed the card John Corbett and gave his last Chicago address.

"Three-sixteen," the clerk said. He laid a key on the counter. "And that will be five dollars in advance."

As Jackson took his money from his pocket, the small radio on the counter began to squawk softly . . . *Calling all cars . . . calling all cars. This is a repetition . . .*

The clerk explained. "It's tuned in to the police band. Sort of keeps me awake.

Then, too, there are a lot of hotels being stuck up nowadays and the boys seem to hit four or five in one neighborhood before they move on. This way I know if anyone's working this section of the city."

Jackson laid a twenty dollar bill on the counter. "And if they are?"

"I've a gun," the clerk said simply.

"Oh, I see."

The radio continued to squawk:

. . . Reminding all cars to be on the alert for Jackson. . . . He may be in any section of the city . . . Pay attention. He is thirty-five years old, five feet eleven inches tall, weighs about one-eighty. Black hair streaked with gray. Deeply tanned from working on the prison farm. Smooth shaven. It is believed, however, his face may be marked from the struggle in the cab. When last seen, he was wearing a smartly tailored but outmoded black Chesterfield overcoat with velvet tabs and a fawn-colored beaver hat . . . This

man is believed to be armed . . . This man is believed to be armed. Code 32. This is an order. P.D.C.

The youthful clerk laid Jackson's change on the counter gently. He looked like he was about to cry.

Jackson thrust his right hand in his overcoat pocket, "I'm sorry, son."

The clerk found his voice. "Yeah. So am I. What is it, fellow?" It was an effort for him to talk. He looked at the bulge in Jackson's overcoat then away. "A stick-up?"

Jackson shook his head. "Uh uh." The combined vowel and consonant reminded him of the Deacon. "Just do what you're told to do. Don't try to be a hero and you won't get hurt."

The clerk wanted no part of trying to be a hero. "Yes, sir."

Jackson picked his change and the sack of sandwiches from the counter. "What floor is the linen closet on?"

"The second floor."

"Let's go up and look at it."

In the small room on the second floor, Jackson ordered the clerk to lie on the floor face down. He tied his hands and feet with towels then picked a third towel from the neatly stacked linen. "I'm going to have to gag you, son. But I meant what I said in the foyer. Don't try to be a hero. Stay put for at least half an hour and you won't get hurt."

With the clerk tied and gagged, Jackson set the spring lock and closed the door. Alone in the hall, he realized for the first time that his entire body was drenched with sweat. He felt like he was walking on water. I'd make a hell of a crook, Jackson thought. He wiped his wet face on the equally wet sleeve of his snow-sodden overcoat and climbed the stairs to the fourth floor.

Room 410 was at the end of the hall in the front of the building. The door was white and set flush with the wall. There was no transom. Jackson looked for the red exit light denoting a fire escape and found it right over his head. If his description was on the air, it could be the waitress in the restaurant across the square hadn't been unobservant, merely poker-faced. Then there were the Deacon and Flip to consider.

Taking his hand from his empty pocket, the big man walked down the hall and rapped lightly on the door of Room 410.

It opened almost immediately. "I thought you were never coming," Olga said. Then she saw it wasn't Thelma and began to cry.

Jackson looked at the weeping child for a long time. Her taffy-colored hair stood out in twin braids from her head; her plump little body was sheathed in a warm-looking woolen union suit; her freckled cheeks were stained with tear-smeared rouge and powder. But the resemblance to Thelma was startling. She could only be Thelma's kid sister, one of those change of life babies that come along to confound the best of families.

He walked into the room and closed the door. "Please, honey," he said, quietly. "Don't cry. It's going to be all right. Thelma sent me." He tossed the sack of sandwiches on the bed and found his handkerchief and kneeled down in front of the child. "Come on now, honey. Blow hard."

Olga blew hard but continued to eye him suspiciously. "How did you know where I was? How did you know my name is Olga?"

"I told you. Thelma sent me."

Olga began to cry again. "Why didn't she come?"

"She couldn't."

Olga was tired. She was hungry. She was frightened. "How do I know you're not a bad man?"

Hart looked around the room. "You're all alone here, honey?"

Olga bobbed her head. "For two days now. And I haven't eaten either." She looked very small and very frightened. She sobbed as she nodded at the big stuffed rabbit that sat upright in a chair. "I haven't even had any one to talk to but Peter Rabbit."

Still kneeling Jackson smiled at the

rabbit. "Hello, Peter."

"Hello, Hart," the stuffed rabbit answered him. "Imagine meeting you here."

Olga stared first at Hart, then at the rabbit. Disbelief turned into a wet smile as she looked back at Hart. "Aw. You did that," she accused.

Hart was hurt "Who? Me?"

Olga bobbed her head. "Uh huh. I know you did. A-cause stuffed rabbits, even Peter Rabbits, can't talk."

"Is that so?" the stuffed rabbit scoffed.

Her tears forgotten, Olga squealed her delight. "Make him talk again," she pleaded.

"Later, perhaps," Jackson smiled. He sat on the bed and held the child on his lap. "Look, honey," he told her. "Thelma did send me to you. And I want you to trust me."

Olga's blue eyes searched his face. "But why didn't Thelma come?"

Jackson evaded the question. "She couldn't. Right now, that is. That's why she sent me."

The baby's face lighted hopefully. "Are you the big brother that Thelma went to find?"

"That's who I am," Jackson said.

"That's who he is," the stuffed Peter Rabbit agreed.

Olga clapped her small hands in delight. "You made him do it again."

"Ha," Peter Rabbit scoffed. "He made me. No one can make Peter Rabbit do anything."

Jackson tore open the sack on the bed. "How long did you say you and Peter have been here, Olga?"

Olga told him. "Two night times and two days. An' I'm hungry." Her blue eyes filled with tears again. "It isn't fair for Thelma to stay away so long. Not even to find a big brother." Her small body shook with sobs.

"Here, here," the stuffed Peter Rabbit chided from his chair. "Big girls your age don't cry."

Olga stopped sobbing and laughed. "How do you do that?" she demanded, looking first at the rabbit then at Hart.

"If you're a good girl, I'll show you," Jackson promised.

"And you are the big brother that Thelma went to find?"

Suiting the actions to the word Jackson said, "Cross my heart, spit on my palm and hope to die on this spot."

Olga still wasn't entirely convinced. "But why did it take her so long?"

Jackson apologized both for himself and Thelma. "Well, the right kind of big brothers are hard to find. Some of us are pretty dumb." He unwrapped one of the chicken sandwiches. "But now let's eat this before we talk any more." He set the carton of coffee on the night table by the bed and took the cover off the container of cream. "And here's something to drink with it."

Olga munched hungrily at the sandwich alternating bites with drinks from the cardboard container. Then she spotted the cake and reached for it.

Jackson moved the cake out of her reach. "Uh uh. Not until you finish the sandwich and at least half of the milk."

The warm little body in his lap squirmed as Olga gave him a dirty look. "You sound just like Thelma."

She felt good on his lap, Jackson held her a little tighter. "That's the nicest compliment you could pay me, my dear."

Olga was pleased. "You like Thelma, don't you?"

"Very much."

Olga finished the sandwich and half the coffee cream. "Now can I have the cake?"

"Of course."

Jackson opened the container of coffee and drank it and ate one of the sandwiches while the child was eating the double order of cake. Now that he came to think of it, he, too, was hungry. He hadn't eaten since he had had breakfast in the mess hall at Stateville.

Finished with the cake, Olga began on the second chicken sandwich. "This is just like a picnic," she beamed.

"Without ants," Peter Rabbit agreed.

Jackson set the child on the bed

and ran hot water on one of the face cloths he found in the bathroom. Then returning to the bed, he washed the powder and rouge from her face. It left her freckles more pronounced. She looked even more like Thelma. There were a dozen questions he wanted to ask the child, but the sooner he got her out of the hotel the better. Either Flip or the police might show at any minute. "Now you get dressed, honey," he told her.

Olga clapped her hands. "We're going to where Thelma is?"

Again Jackson evaded the question. "Perhaps a little later." He picked a small blue wool dress and the blue ski suit from the chair. "Here. Put these on now, like a good girl."

Olga was disgusted. "Without my panty waist? How do you expect me to keep my stockings up?"

"I'm sorry," Hart apologized. He found a small white garment on the floor beside the chair. It looked like it might be a panty waist, whatever a panty waist was. At least, it had garters on it.

Olga put it on and buttoned it, then drew on her long ribbed black stockings and fastened the garters to them. Jackson hadn't seen stockings like those in years. "Where did you get these, honey?" he asked her.

Olga smiled, "In Shelby. At the Penney Store." She confided. "That's where Uncle John and Aunt Sonia live. In Shelby, I mean. Only Aunt Sonia is dead. And Uncle John sent me to live with Thelma. Only I losted the address Mrs. Willis pinned to my coat when they put me on the bus." Olga babbled on happily, pleased to have someone to talk to. "But I wasn't frightened. Not very much frightened. A-cause Thelma wrote a letter to Aunt Sonia just before she died. Aunt Sonia, I mean. And she said she was singing songs at the Club Belly. So I asked a policeman where it was an' he told me an' I walked there and Thelma squeezed me an' kissed me when she saw me." The child on the bed sobered. "An' 'en that bad thing happened an' we had to run away."

Jackson paused in tying the little shoe that was half the size of his palm. "What bad thing happened, honey?"

Olga shook her head. "I promised Thelma, hope to die, I'd never tell. Not anyone."

Jackson let it go for the time being and slipped the blue ski pants on the child.

Olga began to cry again. "An' I promised Thelma I wouldn't leave this room until she came back. An' now you are making me dress an' when Thelma comes back she won't know where I am."

"Hush," the stuffed rabbit demanded.

"You keep quiet," Olga told it. "I even called the Club Belly and asked to talk to Thelma. An' the bad fat man where she works wouldn't let me talk to her. All he did was say bad words."

"You called the Club?" Jackson asked, sharply.

Olga bobbed her head. "But I wouldn't tell him where I was. An' he was awful mad."

"I see," Jackson said. He stuffed the small skirt into the elastic top of the pants and buttoned the matching blue coat.

A vague picture was growing in his mind. There was more to this, a lot more than had come out. The aunt with whom the child had been living had died. The uncle had sent Olga to live with Thelma. The child had lost Thelma's home address. She had gone directly to the Club Bali instead and had seen something she shouldn't have seen, something that involved Flip Evans, something serious enough to cause the fat man to fear her. But before Flip could do anything about it, Thelma had snatched up the child and ran. But whatever it was was too big for the little blonde to fight alone. That was why she had involved him, why she was willing to marry an ex-con, why she had insured her life in his favor.

That much seemed fairly clear. The what and the why he could learn later, if he could persuade Olga to talk. Right now the miniature edition of Thelma was too frightened, too stuffed and too sleepy to be coherent.

Olga tried not to cry and cried. "I want my Peter Rabbit," she sobbed.

Hart picked up the stuffed rabbit from the chair and gave it to her. The rabbit put its stuffed arms around her neck and nuzzled her. "Come on, now, honey," it soothed. "You've got to act like a big girl."

Olga didn't want to act like a big girl. Her ski suit was hot and uncomfortable. Now she had eaten, it was an effort to keep her eyes open. She looked at Jackson crossly, "You are adoin' that," she accused. "'At's you who's making him talk. A-cause Peter Rabbit doesn't call me honey and you do."

Hart started to say, "Now look — ," and turned to the window instead.

A car door had slammed in front of the hotel. He cracked the blind and looked down. There was a big black car at the curb. Four men were standing on the snowy walk. One of them was the Deacon with his left arm in a sling. They started into the hotel and stopped as a police siren wailed in the distance.

Hart subconsciously tried to locate the sound. The siren was faint and in the distance. Headed for the hotel? He looked back at the walk. The black car was still at the curb, but the four men who had been standing on the walk were gone.

8

JACKSON picked the sleepy child from the bed and carried her and the stuffed Peter Rabbit down the hall to the glass door leading out onto the fire escape. The metal rail was cold to his bare hand. The open stairs were covered with an inch of snow. At the second floor level he slipped and almost fell.

Olga's small arm tightened around his neck. "Why don't we go down the stairs on the inside?"

Jackson told her. "Because some bad men are in the hotel."

"Are we going to see Thelma?"

Despite the cold, sweat beaded on Jackson's forehead. He got a better grip on the little body in his arms. "Perhaps, if you're a good girl and don't talk."

The metal ladder on the first floor level was raised. Jackson walked out on it cautiously. He hoped the counter balance didn't squeak when his weight forced the ladder down to the alley. It didn't. The fire escape was new. The weighting mechanism was noiseless. The snow cushioned the ladder as it lowered.

The Deacon hadn't thought to post a guard in the back of the hotel. Jackson stood a moment in the alley, looking up at the fourth floor door through which he had just emerged then walked through a narrow areaway to the front of the hotel.

The police siren was louder now, much louder. A foot from the juncture of the areaway with the sidewalk, Jackson stopped and looked at the car parked at the curb.

It was the same car that Flip and the Deacon used to gun himself and Thelma in front of the shabby parsonage. There was no one in the car. Flip wanted Olga badly. All four men had gone into the hotel.

Jackson peered around the corner and looked into the hotel foyer. A well-dressed hood, new to him, was behind the desk pawing through the registration cards. The Deacon and the other two men had disappeared. Jackson presumed they had gone in search of the clerk. He wished them luck and started up the wide boulevard away from the hotel only to stop and return to the dark areaway as the revolving red light of a police cruiser showed through the snow.

The police car stopped in front of the restaurant across the street. The waitress hadn't been unobservant. She had been poker-faced. She had recognized his resemblance to the picture on the front page of the paper. As soon as he had left, she had phoned the police. What was more, the girl had probably watched him cross the square, saw him enter the hotel.

Jackson wiped the perspiration from his forehead with his free hand. In a moment, the police would emerge from the restaurant and cross the square. Finding the Deacon in the hotel would delay them briefly. Then, not finding him, the police would fan out and comb the dark residential streets. They would radio for other cars to assist in the search. A cordon would be thrown around the district. Anyone found on the street would be a suspect. There would be no talking or tricking his way out of the net. And once the police had him in a cell again, there would be no escape this time. God knew what kind of a story the Deacon had told the police about what had happened in the cab. Now, beside Thelma, he had two dead men on his tab, the cab driver and Max Diamond.

Jackson held the little child in his arms a little tighter. "What happened at the Club, honey? Why did Thelma have to run away with you?"

The only answer was the child's rhythmic breathing. Jackson glanced down at the little face. Her long eyelashes plastered to her wet cheeks, Olga was asleep.

Jackson looked at the stuffed rabbit she was still clutching in one arm. "So what do we do now?" the rabbit seemed to ask.

"I think," Jackson told the rabbit, "that we'd better get out of here."

Jackson crossed the ankle-deep snow of the parkway to the far side of the black car and opened the front door. The keys were in the ignition. He got in and laid the sleeping child on the front seat. Then sliding in back of the wheel, he looked first at the lighted windows of the restaurant across the square then in through the glass door of the hotel. The distance was too great for him to see what was happening in the restaurant. The Deacon and Nick Owens, supporting the desk clerk between them, had returned to the foyer of the hotel.

Flip wanted Olga — badly. Blood was streaming from the desk clerk's nose and mouth but he was shaking his head obstinately. The clerk, too, had heard the sirens and he wasn't talking. As Jackson watched, the clerk tried to break away from the two men and the Deacon clubbed him with the barrel of the gun he was holding in his good hand.

Jackson started the big car and driving

without lights pulled slowly away from in front of the hotel just as the police came out of the restaurant across the square. The thought of the scene between the police and the Deacon amused him. The Deacon would be hard put to explain his presence in the hotel.

Three blocks from the hotel, Jackson turned on the car lights and angled east and south toward the Loop. He had to have a change of clothes. Those he was wearing were too easy to spot. He had to hole up somewhere, get Olga to some place of safety, somehow gain her confidence, get her to tell him what had happened at the Club Bali. It was the key to the whole situation.

But whatever he did, he would have to do it fast. Morning wasn't far away. He drove with one hand resting on Olga's small body. Jackson smiled wryly. Yesterday morning, at this time, he'd been sitting washed and dressed in his cell, waiting for the rising siren to blow. Yesterday morning he'd been a single man, an ex-con about to be released on parole, after serving seven years of an unjust sentence of twenty for second degree murder. All he'd wanted to do was kill Flip Evans. Now he was a married man with a family, a blonde wife and a baby sister. He'd violated his parole in a dozen different ways. And the only time he'd seen Flip had been over the barrel of a gun — the gun in the fat man's hands.

He fiddled with the dial of the radio in the car. The chances were, it being Flip's car, the radio was tuned in to the police band. It was. As the station came on the air, the P.D.C. announcer was dispatching more cars to the Logan Square Hotel:

... Cars 26 and 32 report to Lieutenant McCreary, at the Logan Square Hotel ... That is the Logan Square Hotel, across from the Logan Square El line Terminal. ... Car 19 call your station ...

Jackson turned the big car south on

Clark Street. Here and there a neon sign spelled the word — HOTEL — but the majority of the gin mills and the girlie joints had milked their last sucker dry and closed their doors for the night. Under its white blanket of snow the street looked deceptively staid and law-abiding.

Jackson stopped the car in front of the pawn shop where he had pledged his watch and bags. He sat a moment looking at the unlighted window. The old man lived alone in a single room at the rear of the building. He had learned that much when they had worked out the details of the purchase of the gun. There was a dark narrow areaway between the pawn shop and the building next to it.

Jackson drove the car a block on down the street and parked it. Then picking up the sleeping child, he walked back through the snow to the dark areaway and through it to the rear of the building. Olga made small, contented, kitten-like sounds in her throat but continued to sleep, even when he rapped sharply on the back door of the shop.

A moment of silence followed then the old man called, "Go away. Whoever you are, go away."

Jackson continued to rap on the door.

A light showed back of the drawn shade in the window. The back door, secured by a chain, opened a few inches and the old man peered through the crack. "I said go away."

The big man with the sleeping child in his arms shook his head. "Uh uh."

The pawnbroker recognized him. "Oh. It's you."

"That's right."

"What do you want?"

Jackson told him. "A change of clothes and another gun."

The old man shook his head. "I'm sorry."

Jackson shifted Olga in his arms. "You'll be sorrier if I tell the cops you sold me that first gun. You'll be even sorrier if I tell Flip Evans."

The old man cursed him through the cracked door. "You son-of-a-bitch."

The stuffed rabbit clutched in Olga's arm leaned forward and pressed its pink nose to the lighted crack. "He's all of that, old man. And if you're smart, you'll open up."

The pawnbroker wasn't impressed. "And if I don't?"

"In that case," the rabbit seemed to say, "I'm very much afraid that hot as he is, Jackson is apt to break down your goddam door."

The crack of light vanished as the door closed. A chain rattled and the door opened again, all the way this time. Jackson walked into the small untidy room and stood holding Olga. He'd had a vague idea of using the old man's back room as a hide-out but when he had been in the room before he'd been so anxious to get his hands on a gun he hadn't realized how filthy it and the old man were. He couldn't leave Olga here.

The old man fumbled with one of the buttons of the ragged gray sweater he'd pulled over his nightgown. "That's the trouble doing a guy a favor." He was so frightened his hands were shaking. "I've read about you in the papers. I've heard about you on the air. You know what would happen if the cops find you here?"

Jackson nodded. "Yeah. You'd be in a jam a bad one."

The old man looked at the sleeping child. "Where'd you get the kid?"

Jackson told him the truth. "She's my sister."

"So what do you want of me?"

"A change of clothes and a gun."

"For free, I suppose."

"No. I'll pay for them."

The old man was slightly mollified. "Well — ".

Jackson tossed his snow-covered fawn-colored beaver hat on a table littered with dirty dishes. "Say, a dark hat of some kind, size seven and a quarter." He hesitated to place Olga on the rumpled bed. He compromised by taking off his overcoat and putting the child on the coat. "And another overcoat. Any color but black. Better make it a leather windbreaker if you have one. Size forty."

The old man hesitated. "Well, I'll see." He shuffled into the dark store and was gone for a long time.

Jackson waited, rolling an unlighted cigar between his lips, looking at the sleeping child. He wished he were a mind reader instead of a ventriloquist. Somehow he had to gain Olga's confidence, learn why she was so important to Flip. The child had seen something at the Club. What? In most minor matters, Flip Evans was above the law.

The old man returned from the front of the shop carrying a well-worn leather windbreaker with a mouton collar and a narrow-brimmed black hat. Jackson put them on and looked in the grimy mirror over the stained wash bowl. They changed his appearance entirely. His face was deeply tanned from his years of work on the prison farm. His hands were calloused. He looked more like a farmer who'd come to town to sell a carload of cattle than he did like a two thousand a week entertainer.

"How about the gun?"

The old man took a .32-calibered Colt automatic from the pocket of his sweater. "The hat and coat and the gun will cost you two hundred dollars."

Jackson took his cigar from his lips. "Isn't that laying it on rather heavy?"

The pawnbroker shrugged. "I'm taking a hell of a chance. If the cops ever learn you've been here, I go to jail. If Evans learns I sold you a gun — " the old man shuddered and left the sentence unfinished.

Jackson counted ten twenty dollar bills from his thinning roll. The money didn't matter. Both the police and Evans were looking for him. Whatever he did he would have to do within the next few hours. He slipped the clip of the gun to make certain it was loaded then reinserted the clip and pumped a shell into the chamber before dropping the gun into the pocket of the windbreaker.

The old man said, "And don't come

back. Because next time, I won't open the door."

Jackson picked Olga from his overcoat and snuggled her small cheek against his chest. "Okay."

The old man opened the door and closed it and locked it behind Jackson. It was so black in the areaway that he felt as if he were standing at the bottom of a well, being pelted with hard granules of snow. He had to get the child under cover. But where?

Out on the street the wind seemed even colder. He crossed the street in front of the pawn shop and walked past the car he'd stolen in front of the Logan Square Hotel. It was one of a dozen cars parked in the block. He tried to reason as Flip and the Deacon would reason. For all the power and money they had accumulated, neither man was too bright. Even when the car was located he doubted if either man would think of looking for him in the immediate vicinity. Both men would reason that he would get as far away from the car as possible before he holed up.

Under normal circumstances he might. Still either a Loop Hotel or a rooming house was out of the question. Any landlady would be suspicious of a man carrying a small child. Especially a man with no baggage. Any of the first-class hotels were equally out of the question. All of them had security officers, any of whom would see through his inadequate disguise the moment he walked up to the desk.

The morning grew colder and colder. At any moment a prowl car might wail down North Clark Street and stop beside him.

'You, there,' the officer in charge would call. 'You with the kid in your arms.'

Sweat drenched Jackson's body. And that would be the ball game. The gun in his pocket meant instant revocation of his parole. If Thelma died, it would mean at least life added to thirteen years he still had to do. Then there were Max Diamond and the cab driver. Even if he were not sent to the chair he couldn't possibly live long enough to serve all his time. And God knew what would happen to Olga.

He wished he knew the address of the teen-age B girl who had propositioned him in the bar. He would gladly give her twenty dollars to spend what was left of the night with her. And all she needed to do to earn her money was provide shelter for himself and Olga.

Thinking of the girl gave him an idea. A half-block down the street a taxicab had stopped to discharge a drunken fare in front of a red neon sign reading *HOTEL*. The drunk staggered into the hotel. Instead of pulling on, the cab waited with its meter ticking.

Jackson stopped in front of the glass door when he reached it. The hotel was on the second floor. A flight of fairly clean looking stairs led up to the lobby. He pushed the door open and walked in. There was no doubting what the place was. Even in the lower hall, the reek of feminine antiseptic and cheap perfume was overpowering.

128

Jackson shifted Olga from his right arm to his left and climbed the stairs. There was a small lobby on the second floor. The drunk he'd just seen getting out of the cab was staggering down a short hall partially supported by the bare arm of a girl in a diaphanous dressing gown. Another girl, this one red-haired and fully dressed, was sitting on an overstuffed sofa near a small semi-circular desk back of which a thin-faced man was standing. He could hear other girls laughing and talking in one of the rooms opening off the lobby.

"Now," the red-haired girl said, "I've seen it all."

Ignoring her, Jackson crossed the small lobby and sat the sleeping child on the desk. Then, looking at the thin-faced man, he said apologetically, "I'd like a room for me an' my daughter, mister, please. One not too expensive if you got it." He put just the proper hesitation in his voice as he apologized. "I come in from Ames with a load of cattle but my danged truck broke down right after I got 'em unloaded an' I got to git it fixed afore I kin git home." Jackson inclined his head toward the Loop. "I asked in three of them big hotels back there on the other side of the river but they wanted as high as nine dollars, so I thought I'd walk up this way." He laughed self-consciously, embarrassed. "Now, I'm willing to go to four dollars, five, mebbe if I have to, but like I told the fellow at the last place, I don't want to buy a room." He tightened his arm around. Olga. "All I want to do is git the kid in out of the cold for a few hours."

The stuffed rabbit dropped from Olga's relaxed arm as she leaned her forehead against the leather windbreaker and continued to sleep.

The man back of the desk shook his head. "I'm sorry, mister. But — "

The red-haired girl rose from the sofa and picked up the stuffed rabbit. "You heard the man, Charlie. Give him and his kid a room."

The thin-faced man protested, "But, Stella — "

130

The red-haired girl cut him short. "Who owns this joint?"

"You do," the clerk admitted.

"Then give him 101. Give it to him for four dollars."

The clerk shrugged and searched through the drawers of the desk for a registration card. Finally finding one, he laid it front of Jackson then laid a pencil on top of the card. "You'll have to use this, chum. We seem to be out of fountain pens."

Jackson signed the card — Jim Burroughs and daughter, Ames, Illinois, Rural Route 1.

The red-haired girl closed the door to the room from which the feminine laughter and voices were coming. Then she stood looking at Olga rather wistfully. "You've a cute kid there, mister."

"We like her," Jackson admitted.

It was hot in the small lobby. The red-haired girl lifted a lock of damp hair away from Olga's forehead and tucked it deftly back of one small ear. "How old is she?"

"Seven," Jackson beamed. "Just was last month." He counted four limp one dollar bills on top of the registration card. "It was kind of part of her birthday. I mean coming up to Chicago with me." He touched the brim of his black hat. "And thank you a lot, miss, for both of us. It was nice of you to speak to the clerk."

The red-haired girl folded one of Olga's small arms around the stuffed rabbit. "Forget it. Good luck and good night, mister."

Jackson took the key the clerk offered him. "It's that room there in front," the clerk said.

Inside the room, Jackson closed and locked the door. The room, overlooking Clark Street, was large and clean, obviously reserved for the deluxe overnight trade. Sitting the sleeping child on the bed, Hart unbuttoned her coat. He took off her shoes and ski pants and dress and panty waist and stocking. Then snugging her in between the covers, he kissed her forehead lightly, thinking how much she resembled her older sister.

Olga stirred but slept on. Jackson turned off the ceiling light and sat on the edge of the bed patting her shoulder and smoothing her hair until her breathing was rhythmic again.

The neon sign in front of the window filled the room with a red glow. When he was certain that Olga was asleep, Jackson lighted the sodden cigar he was still clenching in his teeth and walked to the window and looked out and down.

A passing police car, its siren mute, left broad tracks in the snow. A second cab parked in back of a cab at the curb and three young men got out and crossed the walk to the door of the hotel. A moment later he heard their voices in the lobby, heard feminine laughter, heard the red-haired girl say, "Sure. Of course I'm working, honey."

Jackson sucked hard at his cigar and gripped the window sill. It was an effort for him to think. He wished he knew if Thelma was still living. He wished he knew what Olga had seen at the Club. He wished things would be different.

He wished he could have met Thelma before she met Flip Evans.

Jackson picked the stuffed rabbit from the chair into which he had tossed it. "What do you think fellow?"

The rabbit leaned forward and its glass eyes looked up, then down the street. "Well, I'll tell you, Hart."

Jackson continued to puff at his cigar. "Yes — ?"

There was another burst of feminine laughter in the lobby. The rabbit swiveled its head, looked at the room door then back at the motionless lips of the man manipulating it. "So far, so good," it confided. "I doubt very much if either Flip Evans or the police would think of looking for the great Hart Jackson in a five dollar North Clark Street — "

"Uh uh," Jackson warned it. "Careful."

The rabbit clapped a stuffed paw to its muzzle. "I'm sorry," it apologized. "But, well, you know what I mean."

Jackson patted at the perspiration on his forehead. "Yeah. I know what you mean."

9

IT was late morning or early afternoon, Jackson couldn't determine which immediately. What sky he could see over the buildings across the street was a uniform gray. His neck felt as if it were broken. He lifted it from the back of the chair in which he had fallen asleep and looked at the bed. Her chubby body bulging her long woolen underwear, Olga was sitting on top of the covers, playing with her stuffed rabbit, trying to make it talk to her.

The child saw him looking at her and smiled. "You sleeped, didn't you?"

Hart unfolded his tall body joint by joint. "So it would seem."

He stood a moment looking down at Clark Street. It no longer looked evil. All it looked was sordid. While he had slept, rotary plows had swept the snow into two dirty windrows. The amount of traffic on the street made him think it was nearly noon. He walked to the room door and listened. There were no voices in the lobby. He walked back and sat on the edge of the bed. "How do you feel, honey?"

"I'm hungry," Olga admitted.

Hart's smile was right. "Yeah. I figured that."

He ran a palm over the stubble on his jowls. Now the merry-go-round began again. The hide-out had been strictly temporary. He couldn't stay where he was. He had to be on his way again. He was a farmer with a broken truck on his way to Ames, Illinois. If he continued to hole up in the room, revolting as the thought was, the good-natured red-haired girl would begin to suspect his motive. And cats weren't limited to looking at queens. They could also call cops. On the other hand, once he was back on the street, especially now in full daylight, the first cop to spot him would pick him up.

"I'm hungry," Olga repeated. Her

lower lip thrust out in a pout. "Besides you didn't keep your word. You said we were going to see Thelma."

Hart patted a chubby little leg. "Yeah. We are. And we'll eat in just a minute."

He wished he knew what had happened at the Logan Square Hotel after he left. He wished he knew if the police knew about Olga. Probably not. The Deacon had gotten to the room clerk first. The youth wouldn't dare talk. And God knew what song and dance the Deacon had given the police to explain his own presence at the hotel.

Olga liked this new brother. He was nice. Her blue eyes searched his face. "Can I have whatever I want for breakfast?"

Hart stroked Peter Rabbit's back. "Anything," the rabbit seemed to say, "as long as you start with oatmeal."

Olga wasn't amused as she had been the night before. "It's you who makes him talk," she accused. "A-cause I've been trying to make him talk all morning. And he wouldn't say a word till you waked up."

Hart combed Olga's hair with his fingers. "Look, honey?"

"Yes?"

"Do you know what important means?"

Olga thought a moment and added. "It's *has* to be. Like Uncle John doing the chores."

"That's right." Hart felt for words that wouldn't frighten the child. "And I can't explain just why, but it's very important to me, to you, to Thelma, that you tell me just what happened at the Club Bali."

Olga said, brightly. " I walked there from the bus station when I losted the address that Mrs. Willis pinned on me."

"And then — ?"

The child continued earnestly, "A man standing out in front, a man wearing like a fancy solider's suit, wasn't going to let me in. But I told him my sister sang there. And he said I should wait but I didn't. When he opened the door of a car for some people who drove up in front, I wented inside an' looked for Thelma."

"I see."

Olga's small face brightened. "An' I saw her, too. She was standing in a bright light singing a song. And when she finished, all the people clapped their hands. An' I walked back between the tables and down a little hall and through the door that Thelma went in. An' it was another hall. An' I opened another door, but Thelma wasn't there either. A-cause it was a kind of an office, like at the Creamery at Shelby, only bigger, an' all the chairs were green leather."

Jackson rubbed at the stubble on his chin again. Unless the floor plan at the club had changed that would be Flip Evans' office. It opened off the same hall that the dressing rooms did. He asked, "And then what happened — ?"

Olga continued soberly. "Two men were shouting at each other, callin' each other bad names. Like the big boys write on fences. Then the fat man did something real bad and the other man fell down an' got all bloody. An' 'en the fat man saw me an' called me a name an' he was going to hit me, too.

But Thelma heard me scream an' she runned in an' picked me up an' she an' the fat man talked loud to each other. An' he was going to hit her, too. But Thelma runned real fast with me right out of the Club Belly. An' we rode in a taxicab to where she lived an' she got some money an' some clothes an' we went to that Hotel where I was when you found me an' Thelma made me promise I wouldn't go out while she went an' found you." Olga began to cry softly. "An' 'en she didn't come back an' she didn't."

Jackson lifted her on to his lap. "What was the bad thing the fat man did to the other man that made him get all bloody?"

Olga buried her face on his chest and wailed. "I can't tell you."

"Why not?"

"I promised Thelma I wouldn't tell anyone."

Jackson pleaded with her. "But Thelma would want you to."

The small head on his chest moved

from side to side. "No. I can't tell," Olga sobbed. "I promised hope to die on the spot. An' I don't want to die."

Jackson held the small body tighter. And that was that. There was no use tormenting her. He doubted very much if anyone but Thelma could get the child to talk. Olga had given her word. She'd promised 'hope to die on the spot.'

"All right, honey," he soothed her. "You don't have to tell me."

Olga continued to wail. "An' I'm hungry."

Jackson set her down on the floor. "Okay. As soon as you get dressed, we'll go out and get something to eat."

He paced the floor as she found her panty waist and put on her stockings. One thing was obvious. Flip had finally stepped over the line. The fat man was in a bad jam. He was also vulnerable and both Olga and Thelma were witnesses against him. Thelma had known she was going to die when she had come to Stateville to meet him. She had insured her life in his favor then offered her body in further payment to buy protection for Olga. Because he was a 'right guy.' Because he 'took care of his own.'

Thelma's reasoning had been feminine and almost as simple as Olga's. He had taken a fall for his brother. He was a right guy. He was a square. Ergo, if he knew her, if their marriage were consummated before she told him the story, he would feel morally obligated to look after her kid sister. Jackson smiled wryly as he paced. But it hadn't worked out that way. All he'd gotten out of the affair to date were lumps and a wife he'd never known. He turned and sat on the window sill, watching his wife's sister fasten her garters to her stockings. And the hell of it was, he felt just as obligated, even more so, than if he had gone to bed with Thelma three times a day for a year.

Thinking of the blonde girl that way was torture and Jackson was ashamed of his thoughts. The last he'd heard of Thelma she was dying. Probably now she was dead.

He helped Olga into her ski pants and buttoned the blue fluted coat. Maybe after he'd had a cup of coffee, he could think of something.

There was no one in the small lobby. It still reeked of antiseptic and cheap perfume. The crisp air of the street felt clean and good. There was a white tile lunch-room on the corner. There was also an untended newspaper stand. Jackson dropped a coin in the stand and took a paper before opening the door for Olga.

It was earlier than he'd thought, fifteen minutes to eleven. The noon rush was still an hour away. Jackson ordered oatmeal and eggs and toast for Olga and coffee and toast for himself. When it was ready, he carried it to the table in the back of the restaurant, set the oatmeal and eggs and toast and milk in front of Olga and read the paper as he sipped his coffee. The new headline read: *MYSTERY AT OUTLYING HOTEL.*

A picture of the hotel had replaced his picture. The story was even more garbled than he had expected it to be. According to the newspaper account, a waitress at the Logan Square Terminal restaurant had recognized him when he had purchased some sandwiches to take out and had phoned the Shakespeare Avenue Police Station. The captain in charge had despatched a squad to the restaurant immediately. He had also put the information on the air and Lieutenant McCreary of Central Bureau Homicide, already combing the city for him, had arrived a few minutes after the local squad.

He had been seen entering the Logan Square Hotel. But by the time the police crossed the square, he had already departed after beating up the desk clerk. There was a picture of the badly beaten clerk. The Deacon and his boys had really worked on him. Jackson continued the account.

On scanning the hotel register, Lieutenant McCreary had located a Thelma Winston and sister in Room 410, But the sister, still nameless, had fled, presumably with Jackson, before the arrival of the police and the beaten-up clerk had been unable or unwilling to describe her.

Adding still further to the mystery was the fact that one Jack Watts, better known as the Deacon in local nightclub and gambling circles, and three other men with long police records had been picked up in the net the police had immediately thrown around the district. All four men had refused to talk and were being held for investigation.

Jackson skimmed through the story again. His escape from Central Bureau was detailed. The story mentioned that the Deacon shortly before his arrest on the Northwest side had been involved in an accident that had brought death to two men on the Outer Drive. But nowhere in any of the columns had there been mentioned the fact that Jackson had been in the cab when it had overturned.

There was only one logical deduction. Flip and the Deacon were treading on shaky ground. They had to get to him before the police did. They had to locate Olga.

"You aren't eating your breakfast," Olga complained.

Jackson ate a piece of the toast to please her and turned to the follow-up on page two. There was a small picture of Lieutenant McCreary on the second page, a picture obviously snatched hastily from the files, showing McCreary with his wife and a tow-haired girl about the same age as Olga. The caption under the picture read:

Lieutenant John McCreary, in Charge of Search For Escaped Convict Who Is Accused Of Attempting To Kill His Blonde Wife Of A Few Minutes, Admits Some Doubt As To Hart Jackson's Guilt.

The story quoted McCreary as saying he and his squad had questioned Jackson for some hours shortly before the ex-convict's escape from Central Bureau without being able to shake his fantastic story of never having met the beautiful nightclub singer until she had proposed marriage. More, in the light of further developments, McCreary was inclined to believe him. McCreary had been wise enough, however, to leave the story there. He admitted Jackson had accused two other men of the attempted murder but refused to mention names pending further investigation.

Jackson folded the paper, then unfolded it and looked at the word 'attempting' in the caption under the picture of McCreary. He felt better than he had for hours. If Thelma were dead, the line would read 'accused of murdering.' And if the blonde girl had made it this far, it could be she would make it all the way. But Flip would also be reading the paper. And the word 'attempting' wouldn't please the fat man. For some reason best known to himself, he wanted both Olga and Thelma dead.

Jackson picked the check from the table in sudden decision. He was safe one place as another. "You have enough breakfast?" he asked Olga.

"Plenty. Thank you," she smiled.

Olga scrubbed her lips with a paper napkin and picked Peter Rabbit from his chair. "Know something? I like you."

Her warm little smile was infectious. "I like you, too," Jackson said. "In fact, now that I come to think of it, I've always wanted a little sister just your size."

He paid the two checks, bought a handful of cigars and walked rapidly up Clark Street toward the big black car he'd parked the night before.

Jackson attempted to reason logically. According to the story in the paper, the Deacon had intimidated the youthful night clerk into blaming the beating on him. On the other hand, the Deacon himself hadn't dared talk. He hadn't dared tell the police what he had been doing in the vicinity of the hotel or that he had been outsmarted. More, with the Deacon still in custody, the chances were the car hadn't been reported as stolen. The police were looking for him but as far as they were concerned, Olga was an unknown factor.

Jackson eyed the big car as he approached it. It was just another car parked at the curb. Until he figured this thing out, he and Olga wouldn't be safe anywhere, but they would be as safe in the big car as they would be in a cab or in any other means of public transportation.

Olga's legs were small blue pistons as she tried to keep up with Hart. "Where are we going?" she asked him.

Jackson told her. "To see Thelma."

10

THE day warmed as it grew older. It had been spring then winter. Now it was spring again. The wind shifted to the south. The gray clouds dissipated. A hot sun filled the sky. The windrows of dirty snow heaped on either side of the streets and boulevards began to melt. Water gurgled in the storm sewers. The snow on the unshoveled walks turned to slush.

A good omen? Jackson hoped so.

He drove carefully, observing all traffic rules. It was good to be back in Chicago again. Chicago always reminded him of a capricious woman, now prim, now lewd, now hot, now cold, forever changing her mind, but always young and friendly and almost always beautiful, no matter what her current mood.

He parked in the fifteen hundred block on Harrison, three blocks from the great sprawling collection of buildings that was Cook County Hospital. After parking he sat a moment with his hand on the butt of the gun in his pocket. No one came up to the car. No car pulled in behind him. No police siren wailed. As far as he could tell, no one had been watching the car. No one had followed him from Clark Street.

He got out of the car and lifted Olga out. Child-like, she wanted to splash in the ankle deep slush that filled the walk but rather than allow her to get her feet wet and also to make better time, Hart carried her up the walk.

The child was hot in her blue wool coat. Jackson unbuttoned it and the shabby windbreaker he was wearing. The old man had made a good deal. His own coat had cost two hundred dollars. Hart doubted if the windbreaker had cost thirty dollars new. More, now the weather had warmed again, the camphor and mothball smell was almost overpowering.

He thought, I smell like a walking pawn

shop. The damnedest things happened to a man. All he had wanted to do was kill Flip Evans.

Jackson looked at his reflection in a window. On the other hand, the leather windbreaker and the rusty black hat were as effective a disguise as any he might have schemed up. What with the thirty-four hour stubble on his jowls and carrying the freckle-faced blonde child, he looked like Jim Burroughs of Rural Route 1, Ames, Illinois.

The visitors' foyer of the hospital was crowded with anxious relatives, male and female, white and black, of all races and creeds. All had one thing in common. Someone they loved was in pain.

Olga's voice was small. "This is a hospital," she accused.

"Yeah," Jackson admitted. "It is."

Now that he was where he had wanted to come, he wished he knew what to do. He walked aimlessly with the stream of visitors.

"Is Thelma here?"

"That's right."

Olga began to cry softly. "She isn't hurted, is she?"

Jackson patted Olga's small bottom. "She was, but not bad, I think. That's why she couldn't come to you. But everything is going to be all right."

"You promise?"

"I promise."

Olga stopped crying and her small voice turned fierce. "Who hurted her?" As Jackson hesitated, she added, "I'll bet it was that bad fat man who made the white-haired man fall down and get his face all bloody."

Jackson held his breath in hope that the child would continue. She didn't. Instead she began to cry again. "Honey, honey," he soothed her. Her small body was sweet and warm in his arms. He wished she belonged to him. Then his chin jutted slightly as he realized that she did. He and Thelma were legally married. Olga was legally his little sister. "Come on now, please," he begged. "We don't want Thelma to see you with your face all streaked with tears."

Olga wiped her cheeks with the back of her hand. "I'll bet it was."

"Was what?"

"The bad fat man who hurted her. A-cause he tried to hurt me. An' he would have, too, if Thelma hadn't picked me up and runned."

Jackson walked on down the long corridor, one of the crowd of visitors, without the least idea of where to look for Thelma. He looked in the open doors of the wards he passed considering the new information the child had subconsciously given him.

He already knew that Olga had come to the club unexpectedly. He knew it had been night because Thelma had been singing and the uniformed doorman had tried to stop her. In trying to find Thelma after the blonde girl had finished her number, the child had walked into Flip Evans' office while Flip was arguing with someone, obviously a man because in Olga's own words ... *Two men were shouting at each other, callin' each other*

*bad names. Like the big boys write on
the fences.*

That much he had known. Now he
knew the man with whom Flip had
been arguing had white hair. Flip had
badly injured, possibly killed, the other
man before he had discovered that it
might just be he wouldn't get away with
this one, that there had been a small
witness. In his terror, the fat man had
tried to silence Olga and Thelma had
heard her scream. Thelma had picked
up the child and ran out of the club. The
blonde girl had needed help, someone to
protect Olga. She'd known he had reason
to hate Flip Evans' fat guts. And that was
where he had come in.

In her anger, Olga added still more
information. "But if I'd've had Uncle
John's big gun, the one that stands in
back of the kitchen door, I'd have shotted
the fat man dead just like he shotted the
other man."

Jackson wanted to ask if she had
happened to hear the white-haired man's
name and didn't dare. Olga had promised

'cross her heart and hope to die.' Then he thought he had it. Of course. Fillmore Pierce was missing. He had been missing for some days. The fact was featured in every paper he picked up. Pierce was white-haired. He was also an habitué of the Club Bali or had been. When he had emceed there, the aging playboy had always been underfoot, smelling around every new chorus girl that had been added to the line. And if Flip had killed Fillmore Pierce, he had reason to be panicked. Not even Flip Evans with all his political drag could buck the Pierce millions.

There was a pay phone booth in the corridor. Jackson stood Olga on the seat, looked up a number in the phone book, dropped a coin in the slot and dialed AN 3-4800.

"The Sun-Times," a girl's voice announced.

"The City Desk, please," Jackson said. When a man said, "City Desk" crisply, Jackson asked, "I wonder if you'd be so kind as to tell me if Mr. Fillmore Pierce has been located as yet?"

The man at the other end of the wire chuckled. "Why, yes, he has."

"You're positive?"

"We're positive. As a matter of fact, we're running it in the next edition along with a picture of his bride."

"His bride?"

"That's right. Pierce phoned his lawyer from Florida this morning and asked him to call off the dogs. It would seem all that happened to the old man is another chorus girl. A cutie named Alice Willard out of the Club Bali line." The editor chuckled again. "And according to his lawyer, the old man was sore as hell. He claims all the publicity is interfering with his honeymoon. His eighth or is it his ninth?"

"I see," Jackson said quietly.

The newspaperman sensed a story. "You sound disappointed, friend."

"I am."

"You in love with the Willard dame or something?"

"No," Jackson said. "I merely hoped

the bastard was dead."

He hung up and put a fresh cigar in his mouth.

Olga said crossly. "You said we were going to see Thelma."

Jackson picked her up again. "Yeah. We are."

He stood in front of the booth holding Olga. There was no use walking the corridors. He would still be in the building when the visiting hours had ended. He had to ask someone.

A few feet up the hall a male orderly was loading emptied food carts into an elevator. Jackson walked up to where the man was working. His voice was hesitant, slightly embarrassed. He was Jim Burroughs from Ames, out on Rural Route 1. "Say, I wonder if you'd help us out, friend."

The orderly looked from him to Olga and smiled. "Yeah. Sure. If I can. What's on your mind?"

"I stopped at the desk," Jackson lied, "and the girl there told me where to go, but I guess we're lost."

"What ward are you looking for?"

"That's what I don't know. But we want to see Miss Winston, that girl who was shot late yesterday afternoon."

"You mean that nightclub singer who married an ex-con?"

"What's an ex-con?" Olga asked.

"Hush, honey," Jackson hushed her. He looked back at the orderly. "Yeah, that's the one."

The orderly pointed to a bank of elevators. "She should be in post surgery. Take one of those elevators." He added tardily, "You a relative or something?"

"She's my sister," Olga said firmly.

The orderly patted a chubby leg. "Well, you go right on up then, baby."

The elevator was crowded. Jackson squeezed in with Olga, asked to be let off at the surgical floor, turned to face front and then turned his head again and looked at the faces around him. None of them were familiar. None of the men looked like hoods. Still he had a feeling of being watched. Seven years was a long time. The turnover in hoods was terrific.

159

And what did a hood look like?

It could be he was wrong. It could be there had been a stake-out on the car. It could be that he had been followed from Clark Street. Jackson made a mental note of the individual faces. One thing was for sure. He'd know any male in the elevator if he ever saw him again.

He got off on the proper floor, one of a half-dozen worried relatives. Jackson patted the sweat from his face with his breast pocket handkerchief. It had been his imagination. No one had been watching him. The strain was beginning to tell. He was beginning to start at shadows.

He walked with the others to the door of a long ward and a pleasant-faced nurse whose voice was as crisp as her stiffly starched uniform stopped them. "I'm sorry, sir. But children aren't allowed in post-surgery. They should have told you that down at the desk."

"Oh," Jackson said. "I see."

Olga's lower lip quivered. "But I want to see my sister."

The floor nurse looked at Jackson. "What's her sister's name?"

"Thelma," Olga said.

Jackson added, "The girl who was shot yesterday afternoon."

"Oh, yes," the nurse said. "Miss Winston. Well, she isn't in the ward. She's in that private room at the end of the hall. But I doubt, even so, if you can see her."

Jackson followed the nurse's eyes. The door of the room was open. The bed wasn't in sight, but he could see Thelma plainly in the mirror of the dresser. The back of the bed was raised. Thelma was lying with her eyes closed and her bare arms on top of the sheet. Her straw-colored hair was braided into two long strands that hung down over her breasts. With her face scrubbed clean of makeup, except for the maturity of her figure, she didn't look much older than Olga. There was a huge basket of yellow jonquils on the table beside the bed.

Olga squirmed in Jackson's arms,

161

squealing her delight. "There's Thelma, in that room."

Jackson felt his pulse begin to pound. He'd forgotten how beautiful the girl was. And the girl in the bed was his wife. She'd wanted to be his wife, because he was a right guy, because he was: — *The kind of a guy I used to think I'd fall in love with.*

It was difficult for him to speak. He had to force the words past the lump in his throat. Then they tiptoed out of his mouth. "How is she doing, miss?"

The nurse was frank. "One minute we think fine. The next, not so good." Somehow in her mouth the word wasn't profane. "She was doing grand until those goddam flowers came. Since then she seems to have lost all will to live."

Jackson's throat felt tight. "Who sent them?"

The nurse shook her head. "I don't remember the name and Lieutenant McCreary took the card." She looked at Olga. "You say this is her sister?"

"That's right."

"And who are you?"

Olga answered before Jackson could. "He's my big brother. He came to the hotel and got me last night. The hotel where Thelma left me. And we've been hiding from the bad men ever since."

"I see," the nurse said absently. "Well, I doubt if you can see her, but I'll speak to Sergeant Nelson and — " The nurse realized what Olga had said. She looked at Jackson again, her sharp eyes shaving the stubble from his face, combing his disordered hair and discarding the leather windbreaker. "Now, wait — just a minute," she said. Then walking rapidly down the corridor away from them, she called loudly, "Sergeant Nelson. For God's sake, Sergeant Nelson! Hart Jackson's out here in the hall!"

There was movement in the mirror in the room at the end of the hall. The reflection of a big man in a well-cut gray suit blotted out the girl on the bed. Jackson recognized him as one of the detectives who had questioned him at the Bureau. Then the big man was

163

standing in the doorway of the room and Jackson could see Thelma again. Her eyes were open and one hand was pressed to her throat.

"What's that, nurse?" Nelson called. Then he saw and recognized Jackson. "Oh. It's you."

Jackson stood a moment, undecided, balanced on the balls of his feet. He was tired of running. He wanted to give himself up and couldn't. He had Olga to think of. Thelma had entrusted her to his care. And nothing had changed. The way things stood, it was still his word against Evans'. For all he knew, Lieutenant McCreary's statement in the paper had merely been a suck. McCreary had not believed his story last night. McCreary had beaten the hell out of him.

Then there was the matter of killing Flip. He'd lived with the thought for seven years. And you didn't turn hate on and off like a faucet. He'd meant to kill Flip when he'd walked out the gate of Stateville. He still meant to if he could.

There was a fire door on the far side of the hall. The action was instinctive. Jackson jerked it open just as the big man in the doorway drew his gun.

"No. Not in here," the nurse said crisply. "Don't you dare shoot.

As he reached the first landing, Jackson thought he heard Thelma call but he couldn't be certain. The pounding of his heart in his ears and the thud of his feet on the concrete stairs drowned out all other sounds. He was too busy trying to keep the child in his arms from squirming out of them

Not even Olga liked him any more. He raced on blindly with the little girl beating at his face with one tiny fist and the stuffed rabbit.

"You promised," Olga screamed. "You promised. You promised I could see Thelma."

Women, Jackson thought wryly.

11

OLGA stopped screaming and began to cry. Jackson hoped the firewall led to the basement. The detective guarding Thelma would have alerted the desk by now. All the normal exits would be blocked. He'd been a fool to come to the hospital. Even now, he didn't know whether Thelma was going to live or die.

One minute we think fine, the nurse had told him. *The next not so good. She was doing grand until those goddam flowers came. Since then she seems to have lost all will to live.*

Flowers from whom? And what had it said on the card?

Still he had learned one thing. Lieutenant McCreary had thought enough of his story to post a guard on Thelma.

His lungs laboring, Jackson opened basement door. It opened into another long corridor. Jackson slowed his pace to a fast walk. Still another door barred his way. He tugged it open and found himself in a huge dining room. A small group of white capped nurses were eating at a nearby table. With the exception of the group, the dining room was empty. A few of them glanced up as he strode down one of the aisles, but none of the nurses spoke. Jackson was glad the hospital was as big as it was. It would take time for the alarm to spread.

A pair of swinging doors opened into the kitchen. The kitchen smelled like all institutional kitchens, of stale grease, antiseptic and dishwater. A half-dozen cooks were working at the battery of ranges against the wall. Twice as many women were peeling vegetables, scouring the wood meat blocks and work tables and readying the portable food carts for the evening meal. Closer at hand, a toothless derelict, wearing white duck pants and a soiled T shirt, was stacking dirty dishes in an electric dishwasher.

He dug a red hand into the sobbing

child's ribs. "What's a matter, little girl? Kichy koo."

Olga slapped at his hand. "You leave me alone."

Jackson stood a moment attempting to orient himself then walked at a normal pace toward what appeared to be a service door. It was. Jackson walked out the door and onto a paved areaway.

He could hear the sirens now. The news that he was at the hospital was already on the air. Police cars seemed to be converging on the hospital from all directions. A few feet from where he was standing, the driver of a big bread truck put the last of some wooden trays into the truck, slammed the back door and climbed in behind the wheel. Jackson rounded the truck and climbed in beside him.

"Okay. Let's roll, brother," he panted.

"Now wait just a minute, fellow," the driver began. "The company don't allow no riders. Besides — " He saw the gun in Jacksons's left hand and forgot what he had been about to say. His Adam's apple moved up then down. The blood drained from his face leaving it mottled looking. "Yeah. Sure. Whatever you say," he said.

The frightened driver put the bread truck into gear and drove out of the areaway. A half-block from the hospital, he had to jam on his brakes to avoid ramming a speeding radio car making a skidding left turn against a red light. The uniformed officer sitting beside the driver tapped the siren in rebuke but barely glanced at the bread truck. Jackson watched the police car. It skidded to a stop when it reached the areaway from which the truck had just emerged. The doors on both sides flew open and two alert looking policemen got out and stood with their hands on the butts of their guns, scanning the pedestrians on the walk.

The bread truck driver had lost the light. With the idea of using the car he'd parked, Jackson ordered, "Wait for the light. Then cut over to Harrison and turn east."

The frightened driver did as he was

told. His voice sounded small in the mouth of so big a man. "Them cops looking for you, fellow?"

"Could be," Jackson said. "Slow up in the next block. No. In the block after this one."

The black car was parked where he had left it. Jackson started to leave the bread truck then changed his mind. The important thing was to get out of the district before the police could seal it up.

He settled back in the seat. "Go on. Straight ahead. I've changed my mind." The driver looked like he was going to bawl. "Nothing like this ever happened to me before. I'm liable to lose my job."

"What do you want me to do? Cry?" Jackson asked him.

The over-sized stuffed rabbit had fallen to the floor of the cab. Jackson picked it up and wrapped one of Olga's arms around it. She refused to be consoled. "You promised," she sobbed. "You promised. You promised I could see Thelma."

"I'm sorry, honey," Jackson apologized.

Olga continued to sob. "Don't you call me honey. I don't like you any more."

"I like you," Jackson said and let it go at that.

Another speeding police car passed the heavy low-slung truck; this one was a black squad car. Jackson thought but wasn't certain that he recognized Lieutenant McCreary in the back seat. One thing for sure. He was driving the cops nuts.

The driver stopped for another light and almost stalled the motor. He was so frightened he was in no condition to drive. Now they were out of the immediate danger zone, Jackson began to watch for a cruising cab.

The biggest mistake most crooks make is assuming all policemen are dumb. Jackson had heard the statement kicked around in a hundred bull sessions in the prison yard. And the statement had always amused him, chiefly because the lads who made it were doing time while the dumb cop who had arrested them was still sleeping with his wife or girl friend, drinking beer when he felt like drinking beer and collecting his salary every month.

The truth was, you might beat one cop, but you couldn't beat the system, not for long. Once the alarm had spread through the hospital, the nurses would remember seeing him pass through the dining room. The old man would remember Olga. Someone would remember the bread truck that had just made a delivery. The radio car cops would remember the bread truck that had almost rammed them — and every policeman in town would be alerted for a man and a small girl in a bread truck.

The driver's hands were shaking so badly he could hardly control the wheel on the wet pavement. "How far I got to drive you, fellow?" he asked.

"Not far now," Jackson assured him. He spotted two Checker Cabs parked in front of a saloon on the corner of Canal Street. "You can let us out at the next corner. Then keep right on going. Without even looking back, you understand?"

Jackson had returned the gun to his pocket but the driver knew it was there. "Sure. Whatever you say, fellow. I'll stop on the next corner then pull right on."

Standing ankle deep in slush holding Olga, who in turn clutched the rabbit that was almost as big as she was, Jackson watched the bread truck across the street. Then he opened the door of the first cab.

The driver laid down the racing form that he was studying and eyed his bearded fare dubiously. "Where to, mister?"

Jackson got into the cab and held Olga on his lap. It was an effort for him to think. He had to give some destination and couldn't think of anywhere to go. He said the first thing that came to his mind. "The Field Museum. You know, out on the lake front."

The driver tipped his flag. "Look, chum. You run your business. I'll run mine. I know where the Field Museum is. Only they don't call it that no more. It's the Chicago Natural History Museum."

Jackson leaned back against the leather seat as the cab got under way. He'd been under more emotional and physical strain than he'd realized. It was difficult for him to breathe. His hand was shaking so badly he could hardly thrust a cigar between his lips. Lighting it was out of the question. He couldn't go on the way he was, hiding, running, dodging. It was only a matter of time before either the police or some of Flip Evans' boys picked him up. Still, what else could he do but run?

Jackson thought; If I were some sharp shamus or district attorney or smart reporter on a TV show, I'd think of something clever that would wrap this whole thing up. I'd even get on TV myself. And Thelma and Olga and I would live happy ever after. One Pabst Blue Ribbon or maybe Gillette Blue Blades.

But he wasn't. He'd never posed as

a mental genius. So he'd been a high-priced M.C. and ventriloquist. That came under the heading of talent. All he was was a regular Joe, not any smarter than the average guy on the street, not half as smart as some.

Perhaps the best thing he could do would be to forget about killing Flip. Perhaps the best thing he could do would be to tell the driver to take him to Central Bureau.

Something was awfully screwball somewhere.

Jackson's mind raced on. If Thelma was conscious and could talk, why hadn't the blonde girl told McCreary the truth, that it had been Flip and the Deacon who had shot her?

It didn't make sense and then it did. Of course. Thelma was still afraid to talk. She didn't know he had Olga. For all she knew Flip Evans had the child and she was afraid to talk. For fear Evans would kill Olga.

"The bastard," Jackson breathed.

Olga turned on his lap and looked

at him. Her wet eyes were reproachful. "You said a bad word."

"I'm sorry," Jackson apologized. "I was thinking of the bad man at the Club."

"Oh."

Jackson held her a little tighter. "And I'm sorry, awfully sorry, honey, that we couldn't stay to see Thelma. I wanted to see her just as much as you did."

Olga's eyes searched his. "You did?"

Jackson compressed his lips around his cigar and let Peter Rabbit talk for him. "Of course he did. The big goof is in love with her."

Olga clapped her hands. She forgot she was angry. She laughed, "How did you do that?"

"It's a trick," Peter Rabbit admitted. "But if you're a good girl maybe some day he'll show you."

The cab was in the Loop now. As it stopped for a red light on La Salle street, Jackson saw a small florists's shop on the far side of the street. He rapped on the glass partition. "After you cross the street, pull in in front of that florist. I want to buy some flowers."

The cab driver shrugged. "You're paying the fare, mister."

Jackson carried Olga inside the shop, sat her on the counter and counted his money. The five hundred he'd gotten for his watch and bags was going fast, most of it back to the man from whom he'd gotten it in the first place. The old pawnbroker had nicked him one hundred and fifty dollars for the gun he hadn't had a chance to use, the gun with which he had hoped to kill Flip. Ten had gone for drinks and to the teen-age B girl. He'd spent six dollars for the room at the Logan Square Hotel. He'd spent another four for the room in the North Clark Street joint, possibly ten for food and cigars and incidentals. The gun in his pocket, along with the now useless hat and windbreaker had cost him another two hundred. He counted his money a second time to make sure. He had less than one hundred and twenty dollars left.

The red-haired clerk was politely

impatient. "Yes, sir?"

Jackson pointed to a brilliant crimson and yellow orchid in the display case. "How do those run, miss?"

The clerk looked at his shabby windbreaker and rusty hat. "I doubt if you would be interested in those, sir. That is a Queen Cattleya."

Jackson was wryly amused. Time was when buying orchids for pretty blondes had been a speciality of his. "Yes. I know," he said. "A Cattleya Dowiana Aurea. But I believe I asked the price."

"Fifteen dollars apiece, sir," the clerk said meekly.

Jackson counted forty-five dollars on the counter. "I'll take three. They're to go to Mrs. Hart Jackson. In Room 318 at the Cook County Hospital. As fast as you can get them there."

The clerk wrote the name and address on her pad. "And the card?"

"I'll take care of that." Jackson slipped a flower card from its envelope, picked up a pen and wrote — The Boy Friend and Peter Rabbit and — He looked at the child sitting on the counter. "Can you write your name, honey?"

Olga shook her head. "No. But I can print it."

"That's swell," Jackson grinned. "You put your name right after Peter Rabbit." He explained, "You see, we're going to send Thelma some flowers so she'll know we still love her even if we couldn't see her."

Her small face screwed up in earnest concentration, Olga printed a wavery, unevenly sized - oLgA.

Jackson added another five to the money on the counter. "For the tax and for a special messenger. I want the three orchids there in half an hour."

"Yes, sir," the clerk assured him.

Jackson carried Olga and the stuffed rabbit back to the cab. As he got in, the driver started to say something and changed his mind. He eased the cab deftly into the growing stream of eastbound traffic. Then crossing State Street his curiosity got the better of him. Sliding back the glass partition the driver asked, "There ain't no reason why anyone should follow you, is there, mister? That kid belongs to you, don't she?"

Olga answered before Jackson could. "Of course I do. I'm his little sister."

The constriction returned to Jackson's throat. The small veins in his temples began to throb. He wanted to turn and look out the back window of the cab and didn't dare. "How come you ask that question?"

The cab driver drove under the elevated tracks on Wabash Avenue. "I just wondered. I'm not sure, see, but I think one of the cars behind us has been with us all the way, ever since you got out of that bread truck and climbed into my cab. When you stopped at that florist shop back there, it stopped, too. And now it's behind us again."

It was an effort for Jackson to turn. If he and Olga were being followed, it wasn't by the police. The police would have curbed the cab before it pulled away from the corner of Canal Street.

"The fourth car back," the driver said. "A '53 black Caddy. There. It just swung out."

Jackson rode looking back at the car. He had been wrong about the big black car. It had been a booby trap. Sometime during the night, one of Flip's boys had spotted it and had put a stake-out on the car. He had been followed from North Clark Street to the hospital and the stake-out had seen him get out of the bread truck.

He wasn't even as smart as the average guy on the street. He should have read a later edition of the paper. He should have known that with Flip's political power and money working against him, Lieutenant McCreay couldn't keep the Deacon long. Not on any charge admissible to bail.

"You know the guys?" the cab driver asked.

"Yeah. Slightly," Jackson admitted. "I don't know the lads in the back but the guy driving is named Dave Brey. And the guy in the front seat with him, the one with his arm in a sling, is called the Deacon."

The driver was pleased by his own sagacity. "Yeah. I make him now. He was the guy who was pinched up in Logan Square last night when that crazy ex-con who tried to kill that blonde broad — " The driver looked in rear vision and did what the nurse had done. He removed the rusty black hat and shaved Jackson and his voice ran down like an unwound clock. "Jesus," he mumbled. "Jesus."

Jackson shook his head. "Uh uh. Not in front of the kid."

Sweat beaded on his cheeks and forehead. He patted at it wondering why the Deacon and Dave didn't just pull up beside the cab and empty their guns into it. Then he knew. Flip wanted Olga badly. But he didn't dare take a chance on killing the child on a public street. Not with Thelma still alive. The knowledge that her little sister was dead would remove Thelma's only reason for not talking.

The cab driver turned as meek as the

bread truck driver had. He was almost as frightened. "Look. I got a family, bud," he pleaded. He jerked his head at Olga. "A little girl about the size of her. I can't afford to get mixed up in no shooting. What are you doing to do?"

Jackson took the gun from his pocket and rested it on the frame of the open glass partition. "I have to think," he admitted. "But don't you try to. For the time being, just keep on driving."

12

JACKSON rode in the unlighted back of the cab cradling the small blue-clad figure in his lap. Life was a funny affair and filled with women. If he hadn't met Thelma at the bus stop in Joliet, it was possible that either he or Flip would be dead now. If it hadn't been for another woman, Helene Adele, he would never have done any time. Instead of being an ex-con, he'd probably be a big shot on TV. His name would be in lights. He could stop in any of the bars and restaurants the cab was passing and be welcome. Now he couldn't even stop to buy a drink or a ham sandwich because of still another female, Olga.

Jackson smiled as the driver slid back the partition. It was the fourth cab he had been in since the driver of the first cab had realized he was being tailed. Jackson knew what the driver was going to say

184

before he spoke. It had become ritual.

"Hey, bud," the driver said.

"Yes — ?"

"You ain't in no trouble, are you?"

"Why?"

"I think that black Caddy is tailing us."

"Oh?"

"You want me to see if I can shake it?"

Jackson gave him the same answer he had given the other driver. "Don't bother."

In the first place he doubted that the black Cadillac could be shaken. In the second place, he didn't want to shake it. Now that it was dark, he was ready to do the only thing he could do. It might work. It might not.

"Okay," the driver said. "You're picking up the tab, mister. You want me to keep on just driving around the Loop?"

"No," Jackson said. "I tell you what."

"Yeah — ?"

"There used to be some small hotels on Dearborn Street, north of Division.

Are they still there?"

"They're still there."

"Then drive up Dearborn," Jackson said, "and stop at the first Hotel you come to. It doesn't matter which one."

The driver swung north out of the Loop and Jackson felt on the seat beside him for the articles he'd purchased between cabs. He'd bought a cheap razor and some blades, a clean shirt and tie, some more cigars and a late edition of the paper. He might get a chance to read it, he might not.

He turned and looked out the back window of the cab. Now that they were out of the Loop, the lights of the Cadillac were easily discernible. Always keeping four or five cars between him and the cab, Dave Brey was half a block behind. Jackson hoped the Deacon had enjoyed the ride. He hoped it had jolted hell out of his broken arm.

A half-block north of Division Street the cab driver pulled into the curb and stopped in front of a hotel named The Plaza Arms. "This one all right, mister?"

Jackson looked across the lighted walk. It was a small residential hotel. There was a coffee shop facing the street. The hotel and the coffee shop looked clean. He put the paper bags on the seat into the cheap leather suitcase he'd also purchased and straightened the flute hood and blue ski pants on the silent figure in his left arm.

"Yeah. Sure. It's fine," he told the driver.

He paid the meter and walked on into the hotel. A few resident tenants looked up from their chairs as he entered, then back at their papers. Their expressions were bemused. In this changeable Chicago weather, a man was crazy to travel without either an overcoat or hat. But, after all, it was his own affair.

If there were any bellboys, they weren't apparent. Jackson set his suitcase on the tile floor by the desk and told the female clerk. "I'd like a room with a bath, please. Not too expensive."

The clerk looked at the blue-clad figure snugged against Jackson's chest, started to say something and changed her mind. "Yes, sir." She looked in the key rack behind her and laid a key on the counter. "You want it just for the night?"

"That's right, miss."

"I have one at six dollars."

"That will be fine."

Jackson signed the register — Jim Burroughs and daughter, Rural Route 1, Ames, Illinois.

The clerk raised her eyebrows as she read it but said nothing. When you were behind a hotel desk, you bumped into all kinds of nuts. She put the card away, gave Jackson the key and nodded at the self-service elevator. "When you get in, just press the second floor button. The elevator starts and stops automatically."

Jackson picked his grip from the floor. "Yes, miss. Thank you."

He opened the door of the elevator, put his suitcase inside then turned and looked at the lighted walk. Dave Brey was just turning away from the window. Jackson shrugged as he closed the gate and pushed the button. He might have time to shave but he wouldn't have time to read the paper.

The room was at the end of a long hall overlooking an alley. Jackson laid the tiny figure on the bed and closed and locked the door. He would be glad to get rid of his beard. It tickled.

He carried the suitcase into the bathroom and lit the light. He knew he had forgotten something. It was a comb. Still, it didn't matter too much, not with his Stateville haircut. He took the automatic from his pocket and laid it on the glass shelf over the wash bowl. So far, so good. With the exception of the one driver, nobody had recognized him. If the clerk or the guests in the lobby thought about him at all, they'd thought he was a nut.

He ran hot water in the bowl, then took off his shirt and shaved. It was like the old gag in the army. No one wanted to die, but if one had to die, it was nice to be clean. When he had shaved, he put on the clean shirt and knotted his new tie carefully. When the knot satisfied him, he put on his suit coat again, returned the automatic to a side pocket of the coat, lit the light in the other room and picked the paper from the bed.

He was still front page news, but crowded down to the right-hand bottom corner of the page. Fillmore Pierce's new marriage was being featured. There was a picture of the old goat in a solid square of pictures of his former wives, eight in all. There was also a picture of Mrs. Pierce the ninth, a reproduction of one of the glossy prints of the type that titillated the libido of the visiting and local firemen who paused to look at the display in the lobby of the Club Bali. The former Alice Willard, now alleged to be the ninth animated mattress on which the aging playboy had legally pounded, was a wisp of a blonde with a vacuous smile and almost as much lipstick and eyeshadow as clothing. The caption stated that she had been a chorus girl at the Club Bali, but she was new to the line since Jackson had emceed there. Flip didn't keep his girls long. Some tired of the life and quit. Some married. Some left the line to play house with balding businessmen whose bank accounts had finally caught up with their extra-marital ambitions.

Jackson folded the paper carefully and put it in his pocket as male knuckles rapped briskly on the door. "Ask who it is, Olga," he ordered the figure on the bed.

"Who is it?" a childish voice asked.

"You know damn well who it is, Hart," the Deacon said. "Now come on. Open this door before we bust it down."

"Uh uh," Jackson said. "And get myself killed? No, thank you."

The childish voice added, "Go away, bad men. I know who you are. You're the one who hurted Thelma."

On the other side of the door the Deacon said, "Okay. Bust it in, fellows. Be as quiet about it as you can, but we've got to get that brat and get out of here."

A heavy body lunged against the door. The wood splintered around the lock and the youthful hoodlum, unknown to Jackson, lurched into the room, followed by the Deacon and Dave Brey.

Jackson stood with his right hand in his coat pocket.

Brey stopped just inside the room. "Watch him, fellows," he warned the other men. "Hart's making like he has a gun. Could be that he has."

The Deacon's face was gray with pain. "So he has a gun. We have three of them." He cast a venomous look at Jackson. "Before I'm through with him, I'll make the bastard wish he'd never been born."

"What's the mater with your arm, Jack?" Hart asked pleasantly. "Nothing trivial, I hope."

"The guy's crazy," Brey said. "No one but a crazy man would ride around in cabs all afternoon then make it this easy for us to get the brat."

The Deacon nodded at the tiny blue-bonneted, blue-coated and blue-panted figure on the bed. "Get the kid, Dave. Then you're coming to the Club with us, see, Hart? Flip wants to talk to you."

"I want to talk to Flip," Jackson admitted.

Brey strode to the bed and picked up the tiny figure. Then he pushed back the fluted blue bonnet and swore softly as he looked into the glass eyes of the child-sized Peter Rabbit. "What the goddam hell?"

"Ooh," the rabbit seemed to say. "You said a naughty."

Brey dropped the stuffed rabbit as if it had bit him.

The Deacon's face was even grayer than it had been. "Once a wise guy always a wise guy, right up to the end, eh?" His thin lips were an unpleasant slash in his poker face. "All right. Let's have it. How did you get rid of the brat? We been watching all afternoon. We seen everything you done from buying razor blades to cigars. Where's Olga?"

Jackson took his cigar from between his lips. "That's for me to know and for you to wish you knew." The snout of the automatic in his pocket made an ugly bulge as he thrust it against the cloth. "But I believe you mentioned the Club. Shall we go, gentleman? Or would you would-be baby killers rather be mowed down right here?"

Brey started to reach for his gun in his shoulder holster and stopped, holding his hands out and away from his body as if he wished they didn't belong to him. "The guy means it."

Jackson returned his cigar to his lips and enjoyed it. "I never meant anything more," he assured Brey.

The exterior of the Club Bali hadn't changed. A square white barn of a building, its two stories were dwarfed by the surrounding tall apartments and apartment hotels of the so-called Chicago Gold Coast. At the turn of the century before the arrival of the automobile, it had been a riding academy and a livery stable. It hadn't changed in either respect. Only now its fillies had two legs.

A doorman in a crimson uniform heavily ornamented with gold was standing in front of the spotlighted artificial palm tree flanking the door. Even in the evening the parking lot across the street was filled with cars. Every time the door opened the hot strains of a name band filled the walk. If it were later and one listened closely, one could sometimes hear the faint click of the ivory balls in the spinning wheels on the second floor. The Club Bali seldom reached full swing until after midnight. From three until four every morning, the Club was on the air with its own program, The Rounders' Lullaby. Evans' business policy was simple. He catered to the wealthy venal. He sold anything — for a price.

As he braked in front of the club, Brey asked not very hopefully, "You want me to drive around in back to the service entrance, Hart?"

"No. This will do fine," Jackson said. "But let's get one thing straight before we go in."

"What's that?" the Deacon asked.

"There are four of you and one of

me. Anytime you want to risk it, you probably can take me. But my gun will be empty when you do. Remember, I haven't a thing to lose. The least that can happen to me is for my parole to be revoked. And I'm not spending thirteen more years in Stateville. Besides, if I happen to be killed during the exchange of shots, you may never know where Olga is until she testifies against Flip in court." Jackson needled Watts. "And I imagine you were an accessory to that little deal, weren't you, Jack?"

"You're telling the story," the Deacon said.

The uniformed doorman crossed the walk and opened the door of the car. Then seeing Jackson, he backed toward one of the palm trees and a phone Jackson knew was concealed in the branches of the tree.

"Uh uh, Monk," Jackson warned the doorman. "No reception committee. I've got enough odds against me now."

He shot through the pocket of his coat and the slug whined off the sidewalk an inch from the doorman's foot and ricocheted off into the night.

"Geez. I wasn't. I never – " the doorman began. He had to swallow before he continued. "I never done nothing to you, Hart."

"That's right," the former M/C. of the Club Bali admitted. "Flip is the boy I'm after." He gestured with his left hand. "After you, gentlemen."

The Deacon shrugged and led the way into the Club. Jackson followed closely behind Brey. He had no illusions. He knew the odds were against him. Yesterday morning it wouldn't have mattered. He had intended to kill Flip if he went to the chair for it. But now death wasn't so sweet. He had Thelma and Olga to think of. Flip Evans' fat face kept becoming confused with a pair of blue baby eyes and a white oval face framed by straw-colored braids. It could be he could make a deal with Flip. If it would take the heat off Thelma and Olga, he would.

Pierre, the headwaiter, immaculate

in white tie and tails, unhooked the velvet covered chain that kept out the unmoneyed *hoi polloi*.

"Welcome home, Hart," he smiled.

"Hello, Pierre," Jackson said.

The headwaiter looked at the Deacon. "We want to see Flip," Watts said. "There's been a little mix-up. The big boy in his office?"

"Waiting," Pierre said. "If you gentlemen will follow me." He turned and walked down the narrow dimly lighted lane that separated the booths against the wall from the banks of tables surrounding the small dance floor.

Jackson hesitated briefly. He wished the big room weren't so dark. Still, even as early as it was, there were sixty or seventy couples in the Club. Flip wouldn't dare to pull any rough stuff in the open. It would be bad for business.

"Follow Pierre," Jackson told Watts.

The five men followed the headwaiter. None of the couples in the booths or at the tables paid any attention to them.

They were too busy holding hands and each other, planning a big evening.

The place sickened Jackson. Fat old brokers and professional and businessmen pawed at and rubbed high-breasted, hard-eyed young girls and called it dancing. Cheaters kissed in the darkened booths. An older woman was simpering at something her escort, half her age, said. A lesbian was petting her date openly. The whole place reeked of sex and sexual deviation and perversion. Over all, the drums pulsed throbbingly. It was savage, raw, brutal. Jackson wondered how he had ever stood the fetid air night after night, even for a thousand dollars a week. In comparison, the cell blocks were filled with Sunday school students.

Opposite the last booth but one and directly across from the raised dais of the band, Pierre stopped to speak to a couple at a table and the men behind him were forced to stop. Hart waited impatiently, his hand hot and sweaty on the butt of the gun in his pocket.

"Darling! Hart, darling. You're back."

The voice was feminine and shrill and came from the shadows of the darkened booth in front of which he was standing. Then the girl rose and threw her arms around his neck. Hard young breasts bored into his chest as she kissed him repeatedly. Then her arms left his neck and her hands were everywhere, fondling, squeezing, tormenting.

"Oh, I am so glad to see you again."

To the best of his sober knowledge, Hart had never seen the girl before. He'd known it for what it was the moment she'd spoken. He tried to back away from her and draw his gun and someone struck him from behind so hard he could feel his knees buckle.

Evan's voice was hot in his ear, so close that Jackson could feel the other man's lips move. "So you thought you were going to walk right in and shoot down the big old fat boy, eh?"

The sand-filled leather sap landed back of Jackson's ear again. He fought a wave of sudden vertigo and staggered toward the booth.

"No," he heard Pierre whisper. "Keep him out of the booth."

But the headwaiter spoke too late. Brey and the Deacon already had him in the booth. Practiced hands tore the gun from his pocket and beat his sore face to a pulp.

Then he heard Flip again. "No, you damn fool," the fat man reproached the Deacon. "Don't kill him. We'll both go to the chair if you do. Wait till we find out what he did with the brat."

"Back in your office?"

"No. Let's take him downstairs."

Barely conscious, Jackson attempted to cling to the comparative safety of the booth and the girl who had been crowded into the booth ahead of him spiked him where it hurt the most with the high French heel of her shoe.

"Why, you nasty old thing," she said loudly enough to be heard over the music. "I'm not that kind of a girl."

Jackson wanted to scream and couldn't. His pain was too intense. Then Brey's palm was clamped over his mouth.

A man at one of tables asked, "What happened, Mr. Evans?"

The fat man's voice was smug. "Just a drunk, that's all. He tried to get fresh with his girl in one of the booths and it would seem she wasn't that kind."

"Yes. I heard her," the woman at the table said.

Flip continued down the aisle. "Okay, boys. Take Mr. Jones out to his car and one of you drive him home. And tell him we don't want any more of his trade. And you, Pierre — "

"*Oui, monsieur* — ?"

"Don't ever let him into the Club again. We don't need his kind of business."

"*Oui, Monsieur Evans.*"

Smooth, Jackson thought. That was the way Flip operated. He had been a fool to think he could buck him. He opened his mouth in one last attempt to call for help and Evans swung the sap deftly.

"Hush, sucker. Shut up."

A wave of pain reached up and

engulfed Jackson. He thought: As a gunman I'm a damn good ventriloquist.

Then the wave carried him down into a cool green depth and everything was silence.

13

THERE was a dank earthy smell in his nose and Flip Evans' face was a fat and evil moon hovering over him when Jackson regained consciousness. He tried to sink back into the silence from which he had ascended. He didn't want to be conscious. He knew what was coming.

Evans used a fat thumb to pry open one of Jackson's eyes. "Uh uh. No playing possum. I seen you open your eyes."

The sharp pain in his eyeball cleared Jackson's head slightly. He lay looking up at the man, wondering where he was. Then he saw a sack of potatoes and realized he was in the basement room where the produce for the Club Bali was stored.

Evans swore softly. "Now, ain't this a hell of a mess? Damn the parole board to hell. I laid plenty on the line to have you kept tucked away until you rotted."

It was an effort for Jackson to talk. His voice sounded rusty. "I'm sorry."

"Once a wise guy always a wise guy" Dave Brey parroted Evans.

Jackson lay, trying to think what he knew about Evans. He knew plenty. The fat man was a former big-time stagehand who had read the talkies' handwriting on the wall and gotten out of his legitimate racket while the getting was still good and gone into muscle work. That had been years ago. If in the intervening years, there were any of the Ten Commandments the fat man hadn't broken, it was strictly an oversight. A good back slapper and an unscrupulous politician, he had perjured, entertained and procured his way to a fortune. His favorite way to gain a hold on a man he thought he might sometime need was to get him drunk and then introduce him to some tasty little tidbit who just *happened* to be under the legal age limit. There was never any mention of blackmail but a respectable, married judge or ward committeeman or alderman or high ranking police official who had spent an amorous night with one of Flip's fifteen-year-old chorus girls wasn't apt to refuse a favor to the man who knew the facts. Men whom he couldn't blackmail he bought. And once a man had taken Flip's money, he was hooked.

On the other hand, Jackson knew of only three incidents when the fat man had killed or attempted to kill. One was Helene Adele for whose murder Jackson had served seven of a twenty year sentence for second degree murder. The beautiful nightclub singer, while still Flip's unwilling mistress, had fallen in love with his kid brother, Jerry. Flip had beaten the girl to death in such a way as to pin the blame on Jerry, if Hart hadn't stepped in and taken the rap.

Another was the attempt on his own and Thelma's lives. The third was the white-haired man. In Olga's words: *Two men were shouting at each other, callin' each other bad names. Like the big boys write on the fences. Then the bad man*

*did something real bad and the white-
haired man falled down an' got his face
all bloody.*

In view of the attempt on his own and
Thelma's lives and Flip's determination
to stop the lips of the small witness,
there was only one thing it could add
up to — murder.

Jackson sat erect with an effort and
leaned against a potato sack.

"Well, big Sir Galahad come back to
life again," the Deacon jeered. "Let's see
you break out of here, fellow. Let's see
you even try to throw your voice out."

Jackson felt the back of his head.

"Sore, huh?" Evans asked. "Well, it's
going to be sorer before you stop feeling
pain." He lit one of the specially made,
initialed, Turkish cigarettes that he
affected. "So you thought you were
going to walk right in and shoot down
Flip Evans, eh? Just like that."

"Just like that," Jackson agreed.

"The guy's a sorehead," Dave Brey
said. "And why, I ask you? Just because
he picks up seven years that don't belong

207

to him. How was the food in Stateville, Hart? They still serving on a shingle every Thursday?"

Jackson eased his back into a more comfortable position. "Every Thursday."

The fat nightclub owner was the perfect host. "Give the guy a drink. He sounds dry."

One of the hoods whom Jackson didn't know handed him a pint of bonded bourbon. He unscrewed the cap and lifted the bottle to his lips only to have the Deacon kick it out of his hands. The bottle smashed against the concrete wall of the dirt-floored storage room.

"I'm sorry," the Deacon apologized. "My foot must have slipped. I meant to kick your teeth in."

"Okay," Evans said. "Start talking. What did you do with Olga?"

"Olga?" Jackson asked.

"He's going to be tough," Brey warned.

"I expected that," Evans said placidly. "After all, in his own line Hart is a big shot. But if he doesn't talk here after we close in the morning, we'll take him up to the penthouse and he'll throw his voice all over the place before we get through with him."

"Why not work on him here?" the Deacon asked.

The fat man shook his head. "Uh uh. Not after what happened here last week. Use your head, Jack. The guy is as hot as a strip teaser with itching powder on her G-string. Some nosy downtown squad might bust in just while we were having fun. Besides, I don't trust that guy McCreary. You read what he said in the paper."

"Yeah," the Deacon said glumly. "Hart names us to the guy as the lads who gun Thelma and in the light of further developments, McCreary is inclined to believe him."

One of the hoods new to Jackson said, "It didn't say that in the paper. I mean that McCreary thinks you and Flip gunned the blonde."

"That's what it meant." Flip said. "That bastard never has liked me."

"Why don't you fix him, Flip?" Brey asked.

The nightclub owner spread his hands, fat palms up. "How? The fool *likes* to live on his salary. He *likes* to sleep with his own wife. Hell. Don't think I haven't tried to get the guy. Way back before he was on homicide, when he was still on the morals squad, I managed to plant a hot little number on him once, a well-stacked little broad most men would give the left one to go to bed with and what do you think happened?"

"What?"

"Instead of pushing her over like any normal guy would, booked her as a juvenile delinquent. He had her sent to the House Of The Good Shepherd for six months. Then all the time she was there, either he or his wife visited her every visiting day. And when she got out, the little broad chumped off. She got a job working in some office. And the last I heard of her she was married to some square and had three kids."

"How sad," Jackson said.

Evans slapped him without heat. "Okay. Start talking. Hart. What did you do with Olga?"

Jackson tried to steel himself against the beating he knew he was going to have to take. "Wouldn't you like to know?"

"Yes. Very much," Flip admitted. "Look. You waltzed the kid out from under the boys' noses at the Logan Square Hotel last night. You managed to hole up with her somewhere until morning. But you were followed from North Clark Street to the hospital. We know you tried to see Thelma. You were seen climbing out of that bread truck and into a cab. We know you stopped at a Loop florist and sent the new Mrs. Hart Jackson three orchids." The fat man grinned. "With a card which read 'The Boy Friend, Peter Rabbit and Olga,' Olga printing her name herself." Evans' grin widened. "And, by the way, the flowers never arrived. Along with that card, they might have given Thelma the wrong idea. She might have thought it wasn't necessary to protect her kid sister any longer and talked to one of Lieutenant McCreary's stooges. So the Deacon had one of his boys tap the messenger lightly and the flowers and the card are up at the penthouse now. I got a big bang out of looking at them while I was eating supper." Evans continued, "Okay. So you're smart. So the boys fell for the gag of you putting that kid's ski pants and coat and bonnet on that goddam stuffed rabbit when you changed cabs." The fat man slapped Jackson so hard his head rang. "Talk. Where did you have that first cab driver take Olga?"

Jackson wiped a trickle of blood from his lips. "That's for me to know and you to find out."

Evans slapped him again. "We'll find out. This is just the preliminary, fellow. Wait until we really go to work on you. We'll get you to talk if we have to beat your brains in. Why not make it easy for yourself? You haven't a chance."

"That can be," Jackson admitted. He wiped at the blood on his lips again. "On the other hand, you don't dare kill me until you learn where Olga is."

"Don't bank on that," Evans warned him. "The kid maybe could cause me trouble, a lot of trouble. But when it comes right down to it, it's my word against hers."

But the fat man wasn't as confident as he sounded. Jackson could tell by the slight hesitation in his search for words. Flip, for all his money and his political power, was just another fat boy whistling in the dark. The law of averages was against him. His luck couldn't hold forever. Sooner or later he had to take a fall.

Evans added, "Besides, the police can't prove a goddam thing without a body."

For some reason the remark amused the Deacon. He laughed, then said, "Let me go to work on him, Flip. I owe the bastard plenty for wrecking that cab and breaking my arm."

"Later, maybe," the fat man said. He took off his coat. "Right now, it's my party. I never did like Hart, even when he was working for me. He was

213

always so goddam superior. Then when he took the fall I'd arranged for Jerry, that cooked it. The only noble guy I ever liked was a crooked polack ward heeler who used to hand out at the Noble Street A.C."

He gripped Jackson's hair with his left hand and slapped him, first with the palm, then with the back of his right hand, drawing blood with both blows. "How much did the kid tell you, Hart?"

"Plenty," Hart panted.

"The little bitch *would* come in when she did. And me so mad and her so small I didn't even see her." He repeated the treatment. "Okay. What did she tell you?"

"She said she saw you argue with, then kill a man. In your office."

"Did she describe him?"

"Yes."

"What did he look like?"

"She said he had white hair."

"How did I kill him?"

"You shot him," Jackson said flatly.

"He knows, all right," the Deacon said.

Flip Evans doubled his fist and hit Jackson as hard as he could. "Talk. Where did you have that first cab driver take Olga?"

The blow knocked Jackson back against the sack of potatoes against which he had been sitting. His jaw felt like it was fractured. He tried to tell Flip to go to hell and couldn't. His mouth was too filled with blood. His body was too filled with pain. He sat up and was sick on the dirt floor.

Evans stepped back a few feet. "Not on my pants leg, punk." He looked at the Deacon. "Hart's going to make it tough on himself. I can see that right now. How come you fell for such a gag? How come you couldn't tell it was the kid's stuffed rabbit he was carrying?"

The Deacon defended himself. "How could I? They're both about the same size, the rabbit is wearing the kid's clothes and we're not close enough to

215

see her face. If you'd let me rub them both out like I wanted to, we wouldn't be in this mess. But no. 'Don't pull anything on the street.' you tell me. 'We're hot enough as it is. Wait until Hart holes up again, then take them.'"

Dave Brey stepped in between Evans and the Deacon. "All right. Take it easy. Fighting among ourselves isn't going to get us anywhere. All we got to do is make Jackson talk."

"That's all," Evans agreed. He didn't sound too hopeful.

He turned his head as Pierre entered the storeroom. "You'd better get upstairs, Flip," the headwaiter said. "Our wire at H.Q. just called and it would seem that all hell has busted loose."

The fat man put on his coat. "What now?"

Pierre told him, without even a trace of a French accent. "For one thing it seems the Winston dame wasn't as badly wounded or as weak as they thought she was. About half an hour ago, when the police guard stepped out

216

of the room to go to the john, she climbed out of bed and disappeared. At least, they can't find her in the hospital."

Evans swore under his breath.

"Is *that* all?" The Deacon said. He leaned on the word that.

"No," Pierre told him. "Lieutenant McCreary and his squad are on their way over here. What's more, they have a search warrant."

Watching Evans' face, Jackson saw it turn a fish-belly white. "What do they expect to find?" Evans asked.

Pierre shrugged. "Our wire at H.Q. didn't know."

The fat man saw Jackson looking at him and kicked him in the face. "You two-voiced bastard. This is all your fault. Why didn't you stay in the can where you belonged?"

Dave Brey was as frightened as Evans was. "So what do we do with Hart?"

Evans kicked Jackson again, on the point of the chin this time. "I'll take care of that little matter. To a cop one sack of potatoes looks exactly like another."

"Sure," the Deacon said, poker-faced. "I get it. We got away with it once. Could be it will work again."

He didn't sound too confident.

14

THE earthy smell continued. There was a great weight on his chest. His swollen tongue filled his mouth, making breathing difficult. Jackson realized his lungs were laboring, still only inhaling a minimum of air.

With returning consciousness, he knew panic. He thought: The bastards. They've buried me. They've buried me in the produce cellar.

He thrust upward with his chest and met an immovable weight. His panic made it more difficult for him to breathe. Then reason asserted itself. Flip didn't want him to die. Flip couldn't afford to have him die, not until he was forced to tell what he had done with Olga.

Jackson lay breathing quick, shallow breaths, waiting for his head to clear from the effects of Flip's last kicks. He was still in the produce cellar. That much he knew. He was lying on dank earth. And the weight pressing him into the ground were God knew how many sacks of potatoes. He could feel the rasp of a rough burlap bag on his face when he moved his head from side to side.

Jackson forced himself to think. He knew now who was dead, whom Olga had seen Flip kill. He wasn't the first man to be hidden in the cellar. What was it Flip had said?

I'll take care of that little matter. To a cop one sack of potatoes looks exactly like another.

He explored the object in his mouth. His tongue wasn't swollen. The object in his mouth was an unwashed potato. He could taste the earth and the skin. A small potato had been stuffed into his mouth and tied in place with a towel or a piece of rag. His hands were bound behind his back. He tried to move his legs. He couldn't there was no sensation in them.

Jackson turned his head to one side and found he could see a small section of the cellar through a half inch wide zig-zag tunnel in the sacks heaped on top of him. The cellar was lighted. The door leading into it was open. In his own way, Flip was smart. He knew police psychology. The police seldom investigated the obvious.

As Jackson watched, there was a scuff of feet on the cement floor outside the cool room. A pair of dirty white duck pants legs became a kitchen helper wearing a T-shirt and a soiled white blood-stained apron. The man was carrying a hatchet. He used it to hack off the top of a barrel containing frozen chickens. As he pried each chicken out of the barrel, he laid it on a dirty tray.

Jackson was wryly amused. If the wealthy patrons of the Club Bali who paid from five to ten dollars for *Poulet aux Champignons Frais* or *Poulet Chanteclair* or *Poulet Demi-Bordelaise* could see how their food was handled before it was brought to table, they might not be so enthusiastic about the Club Bali cuisine. Personally he'd always eaten elsewhere.

On the other hand, considering the amount of liquor most of the patrons consumed before they ate, it was doubtful if any germ could live in the sea of alcohol in which it found itself submerged.

The kitchen hand was still digging in the barrel of frozen chickens when other feet scuffed on the cement floor of the basement.

"Go right ahead. Help yourself, Lieutenant," Flip Evans said. "Look in every corner. It says in your search warrant you can. I want you to. But I'll be damned if I know what you are looking for."

"I'll bet," said Lieutenant McCreary, coldly.

Jackson tried to cry out and couldn't. The potato and the towel formed an effective gag.

"What are you looking for?" Evans asked.

"You'll know if we find it," Sergeant Nelson said.

Evans sounded hurt. "Well, all I have

to say is this is a hell of a way to treat a respectable businessman."

"Ha," Nelson scoffed. "A guy learns something every day. That's a new name for a pee-eye."

Evans was even more hurt. "I resent that."

"Resent and be damned," McCreary said. The scuff of feet stopped in front of the produce cellar. "What's in here?"

"Produce," Evans told him. "We call it the cool room. We store our vegetables in here. Also the meat and fowl we move out of the deep freeze to thaw for twelve hours before we use it."

"You," Lieutenant McCreary said.

The kitchen help stopped digging frozen chickens from the barrel. "You talking to me?"

Jackson heard the scratch of a match as if one of the three men had lighted a cigarette or a cigar. "I'm not looking at anyone else," McCreary said, between puffs of his newly lighted cigar. "You see Hart Jackson here tonight?"

"That big good-looking guy? The one

whose picture was in the paper? The one who used to work here?"

"That's the one."

The kitchen worker shook his head. "Uh uh." His sincerity was obvious. "Naw. I ain't seen him." He tried to be helpful. "Jeez. From what I read about the guy, you're looking in the wrong place, Lieutenant, Jackson is too hot to be hanging around nightclubs."

"How about a little seven-year-old blonde girl wearing blue ski pants and a blue wool coat."

"And a blue bonnet," Sergeant Nelson added.

"What about her?"

"Have you seen her?"

"Here?"

"You heard us."

The kitchen helper pried another brace of frozen chickens out of the barrel. "Now I know you're kidding me. No one would bring a seven-year-old kid to a joint like this."

"Answer the man," Evans said.

The kitchen helper lifted the tray of

224

chickens, dropped one on the dirt floor, picked it up, wiped the chicken on his blood-stained apron, put it back on the tray and disappeared from Jackson's range of vision. "Naw, I ain't seen no kid," he told McCreary. "Although I must say," he added, "a dame any age with pants on would be a novelty around here. You ain't got no idea, Lieutenant, what a strain it is on a guy to watch all them pretty quail strip night after night, then have to go home and take it out on an old bag like I'm married to."

Only Evans laughed, "So now I know."

"You know what?" McCreary asked.

"Why the honor of this visit." All Jackson could see through the zig-zag tunnel in the piled sacks of potatoes covering him was one of Flip's legs. The nightclub owner was amused. "You've been transferred back to the morals squad and you're looking for Jackson and a seven-year-old kid. Jeez. I know the guy has been locked away from it for some time but he must be hard put to pick on a kid that young."

Jackson heard the smack of a muscular fist on flabby flesh.

Evans grunted in pain. "You son-of-a-bitch! I'll get your job for that."

Lieutenant McCreary sounded tired. "The times that has been remarked to me. And I'm still on the Force. Now let's get one thing straight, Evans."

"What?"

"You haven't seen Jackson tonight?"

"No."

"And I suppose if I were to haul you down to the Bureau, your story would be you hadn't the least idea that Thelma Winston has a baby sister named Olga."

"She has?"

"You didn't know Thelma had a sister until I told you just now?"

"No."

"You didn't know that Thelma checked her into the Logan Square Hotel the night before last?"

"No, I didn't."

"Then what was the Deacon and those other boys of yours doing at the Logan Square last night, right after

226

that mysterious accident on the Outer Drive, right after Jackson crushed out of Central Bureau? Why did they beat hell out of the desk clerk trying to find out what room Miss Winston was in, then scatter when a squad from the Shakespeare Avenue station pulled up in front of the hotel?"

"There you have me," Evans said. "Why don't you ask the Deacon?"

"We did. For hours. And it may be we'll ask him again, as soon as we locate the Winston dame and her kid sister and Jackson."

The nightclub owner simulated surprise. "Locate Thelma? I thought she was at Cook County."

"She was up until an hour ago."

"Now she's taken a powder, too, huh?"

"That's right."

"And you think she and Jackson and this kid sister you say she has are together?"

"Could be," Sergeant Nelson said. "Jackson showed up at the hospital this afternoon carrying the kid sister, see?"

"I'll be damned," Evans said. "I didn't read that in tonight's papers."

"Thelma talked to Jackson and her sister?"

"No," Nelson said. "She didn't even see them. All she heard was the commotion in the hall. But four hours later when the officer who relieved me had to go to the john, she got out of bed and out of the hospital somehow."

"And now you think she and Jackson and the kid are together?"

"Could be."

"Can you beat that?" Evans asked. He philosophized. "Dames are funny. You wouldn't think Thelma would ever want to see the guy after what he tried to do to her."

McCreary's voice was cold. "I don't believe he did."

"Did what?"

There was the sound of another blow. Evans cried out in pain. McCreary continued, weighing his words, "You know damn well what I mean, you big fat slob. Sure. We jumped on Jackson. We beat hell out of him. Mainly because he was an ex-con, she was your girl and he admitted he had a grudge against you. But the more time that elapses, the better his story sounds to me."

"What story?"

"That you and the Deacon gunned Thelma."

"Don't be silly."

"I don't think I am being silly."

"Why should I gun Thelma?"

"She was your girl or had been your girl and Jackson married her."

Watching the fat nightclub owner's pants leg, Jackson saw a steady dribble of blood spatter on the concrete floor. Evans talked like he was holding one finger under his nose in an attempt to stop the bleeding. "You're crazy. What's one girl to me? I got a new one the minute Thelma walked out."

The girl in the booth, Jackson resumed. The one who had called him darling and set him up for the sap by spiking him with her high heels.

"Why don't you ask Thelma who shot her?"

"We did. And first she couldn't talk because she was unconscious. Then when she could, she wouldn't. She was afraid to." There was the sound of still a third blow. "Why? Why was she afraid to talk, Flip?"

"I don't know," the fat man whimpered. "If you think I gunned Thelma, why don't you pinch me?"

McCreary was frank with him. "Because right now I couldn't make it stick. Because there is a hell of a lot more to this than has come out yet. Because I'm waiting on a couple of phone calls. You wouldn't know where from, would you, Flip?"

"How the hell would I know?"

"From Miami."

"From Miami?"

"That's right," McCreary said. "You see I just want to be sure another former girl friend of yours, a kid by the name of Alice Willard, is having a good time on her honeymoon."

Blood continued to drip on the floor. "I don't know what you're talking about," Evans said. "Now either pinch me and let me call my lawyer or stop beating me."

"Okay," McCreary said quietly. "We'll call it a session. This was just a friendly little talk. Sort of a get-together. My fist and your nose. That's all. For now." The scuff of feet on cement resumed as the three men walked away from the produce cellar. McCreary's voice came faintly from the stair. "But I have a hunch we'll be back. And next time we come, we won't give it a once-over-lightly. We'll tear this goddam joint to pieces. We'll take it apart brick by brick."

Some of Evans' cockiness returned. "Looking for what?"

"Oh, this and that," Lieutenant McCreary told him.

15

JACKSON lay for long minutes after the voices and footsteps had faded, attempting to conserve his breath and his strength.

Lieutenant McCreary was one of two things. He was either a very smart cop or a fool.

Police work was never the simple procedure the average layman considered it to be. That much he knew. Unless a man was caught in the act of murder, there were always a dozen different angles that had to be taken into consideration. There were laws pertaining to the gathering of evidence that had to be observed. A smart officer seldom made a pinch at least in the Flip Evans' bracket, unless he was certain he could see it through.

It could be McCreary knew. It could be that in lieu of a *corpus delicti*, the

232

alleged search of the Club Bali, in which no real searching had been done, was a move to feint the fat nightclub owner off balance, goad him into making some incriminating move.

On the other hand, it could be McCreary was dumb. A lot of cops were. It could be he hadn't sense enough to recognize a captaincy when it was delivered to his door.

Still, he had mentioned Miami. He had warned Evans he might return.

In either case, Jackson thought wryly, when Lieutenant McCreary returned to the Club Bali, if he did, it would be too late to do him any good. Whatever was done for him, he would have to do himself.

The weight on his chest was mashing him into the soft loam on which he was lying. The crude gag in his mouth was stifling him. It was growing momentarily more difficult for him to breathe. More, when Flip and the Deacon and Brey dug him out from under his crude hiding place, all he had to look forward to was another beating. Now, with Thelma missing from the hospital, Flip had to know where Olga was.

Jackson bunched his chest and shoulder muscles, thrust up at the weight pinning him down and attempted to wriggle toward the sliver of light.

He couldn't be certain but he thought the piled sacks gave a little, that his weighted body moved perhaps two inches. There was more weight on his head, less weight on his legs. And his legs weren't bound, they were numbed. The effort had caused them to tingle. He tried again, moved another inch, then had to lie swallowing his saliva, fighting desperately not to choke on it, as he sucked air past the gag in his mouth. A million needles were stabbing his legs now. He drew them up as far as he could, dug his heels into the loam and pushed.

This time he knew he moved. There was even more weight on his head. One side of his face was rasped raw by the coarse sacking, but the sliver of light had enlarged to the size of a big man's arm. More, in his haste to get him out of sight before the searching party reached the club, whoever had tied him hadn't knotted the rope around his wrists securely and the movement of his weighted body had rolled the rope down over his hands.

Using his heels for leverage and the backs of his arms as skids, Jackson pushed again and again and, his head and shoulders digging a trench in the soft earth, slid out from under the stacked sacks of potatoes. Another push freed his arms. He tore the gag from his mouth, spit out the bloody potato, sucked his lungs full of air, then had to turn on his side as he was violently sick.

When he could, he freed his legs and got to his feet. There was no stiffness in his knees. His legs trembled so badly from the strain he had put on them that he walked as if he were drunk. He wobbled limp-legged across the produce cellar and had to catch hold of the barrel of frozen chickens to keep from falling.

Jackson clung to the barrel for a long time. Too much had happened too fast. He'd had too little sleep. He'd been under too great an emotional strain. He was no longer thinking clearly. So he was out from under the stacked sacks of potatoes. So what? Now all he had to do was get out of the club, with a party of drunks at every table and one of Flip's boys watching every entrance and exit, not against his attempted escape but against Lieutenant McCreary's possible return. He no longer had anything to lose. If he had been smart, instead of lying on his lean backside, feeling sorry for himself, listening to their conversation, wondering if McCreary was smart or dumb, he should have tried to free himself while Lieutenant McCreary and Sergeant Nelson had still been in the cellar. One of them would have been almost certain to notice movement in the stacked sacks of potatoes. And glib as he was, it would have been difficult if not impossible for Flip to explain it away. There were no earthquakes in

236

Chicago. Jackson looked at the trench his body had gouged in the soft earth. Nor any moles. At least, not in the heart of the city.

He lifted his hand from the barrel. He could walk. His legs were no longer trembling. He filled in the small tunnel with his hands them smoothed the dirt with his feet.

As he tramped the earth solid again, he tried to remember if the basement windows of the club were barred. He glanced up at the one in the cool room. They were. Somehow he would have to go out through the club.

He walked to the door of the produce cellar and studied the cluttered basement. The nightclub owner had the instincts of a magpie. The only things he didn't save were his women. The bulk of the basement was filled with old tables and chairs and kitchen and gambling equipment brought down from the floors above. It was small wonder McCreary and Nelson hadn't made a minute search of the club. It would take a crew a week to go through the litter in the basement. From where he stood, Jackson could even see an upended old concert grand piano and behind it a large fuse box. He eyed the fuse box thoughtfully, wondering if it controlled the lighting for the entire club. As he recalled, there was another fuse box in the hall off which Flip's office and the dressing rooms opened.

The club's wine cellar and liquor vault were next to the produce cellar. There was a small washroom next to the vault. Jackson pushed open the door and walked in. The taste in his mouth was gagging him. He had to rinse it out with something. There was a small yellow-stained bowl in the washroom. He cupped his hands under a cold water tap and drank from them thirstily. The water made him sick again. He lost it but felt better when he'd finished. At least, the taste of blood and rotten potato were gone. He splashed cold water over his face, then looked at himself in the cracked mirror over the bowl.

He no longer looked like a thousand

dollar a week M.C. He looked like a West Madison Street bum. One side of his face was rasped raw from the rough sacking. The back of his once expensive suit was covered with black loam. His hair was matted with blood and dirt. He wanted a drink. He wanted a bath. He wanted to talk to Thelma. He wanted to see Olga again. He was lucky he was alive. More, there was no telling how long his luck would hold out.

He walked out into the basement again. There was a flight of narrow wooden stairs at the far end. Jackson started for the stairs and stopped as the door at the top of the stairs opened. Two pairs of legs appeared, one of them in black evening trousers.

Jackson's flesh crawled. This was it. While Flip played the jovial host for the drunks on the floor above, the Deacon and one of the boys had come down to work on him. He ducked back of the upended grand piano, looking desperately for a weapon.

There was a brief raucous blare of

music. The door closed again. A key turned in the lock. Then the two men descended the stairs.

One of them was the Deacon. The other was one of the new boys, a hood whom the Deacon addressed as Larry. As big a man as himself, Larry was dressed in typical hoodlum finery, a three hundred dollar wraparound camel's hair topcoat, a fawn colored Borsalino and underneath, an expensive dinner jacket.

"*Nouveau riche*," Jackson chuckled to himself.

The two men stopped in front of the door of the produce cellar. "All right, Let's go," the Deacon said. "Get those goddam sacks off him and let's go to work on the bastard. That son-of-a-bitch McCreary may show any minute."

Larry took off his topcoat and hat and dinner jacket and laid them carefully on a stack of discarded chairs. As he did, he laughed. "You sound like you're enjoying this or going to."

"I am," the Deacon admitted. "The big bastard made a monkey out of me.

We tail him for hours and all the time he's carrying a goddam stuffed rabbit dressed in the kid's clothes."

"No luck in locating that first cab, eh?"

"Not so far."

"And Thelma?"

"God knows where she is. I warned Flip against that broad. I knew that sooner or later she was going to cause us trouble. She wasn't 'happy' here, if you get what I mean. Then when Flip pulled that bonehead play of trying to get her to lay Pierce, well, pop went the weasel."

The two men entered the produce cellar. Jackson debated making a break for the stairs and decided against it. He would have to pass the door to the produce cellar. The door at the top of the stairs was locked.

He heard Larry grunt as he lifted a sack of potatoes. "How far down is he?"

"All the way. On the dirt," the Deacon said.

Larry continued to grunt as he shifted

241

the pile of potatoes. Then Jackson heard him say, "What the hell!"

"What now?" the Deacon asked.

"You sure he's under here?"

"Positive. I saw Dave and Jim put him there. Why?"

Larry told him. "He ain't there now. Take a look for yourself. I only got two more sacks to go and there ain't anything under them but dirt."

The Deacon appeared in the door of the produce cellar with a gun in his hand. His eyes moved slowly over the clutter. "Still a wise guy, eh? Some guys never learn. Okay, Hart. Make it easy on your self. I know you're here somewhere."

Jackson stood motionless behind the upended piano. He could see the other man but the Deacon couldn't see him.

The Deacon's eyes continued to move from one pile of discarded equipment to another. "I got to give you credit. You're good, fellow. But you can't get out of the club. You know that. So why not be sensible? Tell us what you did with the kid and we'll let it go at that."

Jackson continued to stand motionless.

The Deacon took several steps into the basement and Larry appeared in the door of the produce cellar wiping his hands on a clean handkerchief. "A smart bastard, eh?"

"So it would seem," the Deacon said. "Take a look in the john there."

Larry opened the door of the washroom and looked in. "All clear in there."

The Deacon backed slowly toward the stairs. "Well, don't just stand there. Start looking for him. He has to be back of some of this crap."

The younger man hesitated briefly. "Has he got a gun?"

"Where would he get a gun?"

"How did he get out from under them potatoes?" Larry countered. He moved away from the door of the washroom, then stood a moment as if uncertain just where to begin.

"Start at the other end and work back this way," the Deacon ordered.

Jackson glanced quickly at the fuse box. The piano hid him from the Deacon but as the younger man walked back down the aisle between the clutter of discarded equipment he couldn't help but see him. When Larry had almost reached the piano, Jackson attempted to open the metal fuse box to get at the master switch and catching sight of movement the young hoodlum quickened his steps.

"Uh uh," he warned Jackson. "That's naughty. Mustn't play with the lights."

"You got him?" the Deacon asked.

"Yeah. He's right here back of the piano," Larry said.

Young, cocky, sure of himself, he closed in on Jackson and Jackson hit him with a short right hook to the jaw that bounced the younger man's head against the upended piano so hard that the wires jangled. He followed the blow with a slashing motion of his left hand.

Larry tried to scream and couldn't. His lips moved but no sound came from his mouth. The side of Jackson's left hand caught him across the throat. His eyes agonized, the young hoodlum instinctively attempted to squeeze the pain and Jackson hit him again. His hands fell away from his throat. His broad back pressed against the piano. Then he slid to the floor.

"What happened?" the Deacon called.

Jackson tried to imitate Larry's voice. "I had to hit him. Come here and give me a hand."

A moment of silence followed. Then a steel jacketed slug bored through the piano and slapped into a discarded sofa behind Jackson. "Uh, uh," the Deacon said. "Don't try to give me that. That's for the sucker trade, Hart. Okay. I've fooled with you long enough. Come out from in back of that piano and come out with your hands up."

Jackson finished what he'd started to do. He opened the metal fuse box and pulled the switch.

The Deacon wasn't impressed. "You wise guys never do get over it, do you? But now let me tell you something, Hart. You think I don't dare shoot you. You think I *have* to know where Thelma's kid sister is. Well, that's where you're wrong. It's Flip who's doing the sweating, not me. I wasn't in on that caper. And now we know the little blonde broad is going to live, the law hasn't a thing on me that I can't beat. Think that over."

The darkness suddenly had weight. Jackson could feel it close in on him. He knew what the other man meant. It had long been a recognized fact that if anything ever happened to Flip, the Deacon would take over. And if he weren't personally involved in the killing that Olga had witnessed, this was as good a chance as the Deacon would ever have to step into the fat man's shoes.

Jackson felt his way out from behind the piano.

"Go ahead. Throw your voice," Watts taunted. "One gets you ten I hit it."

The Deacon sounded closer than he had. Jackson trailed his fingertips along the wall. He felt the closed doors of the washroom and the liquor vault, then the open doorway of the produce cellar.

The Deacon was only a few feet away from him now. "Too bad, Hart," the other man said. "If you had stayed under those potatoes, all you'd have gotten was a beating. But this is too good a chance to miss. So help me, Flip is going to need a diaper when I tell him that I had to shoot you."

The Deacon shot again. Jackson backed away, instinctively, from the stab of flame and one of his heels thudded against the barrel of frozen chickens.

"Oh. In there, eh?" the Deacon asked.

He fired a third time at the sound and the bullet creased Jackson's thigh. He had backed as far as he could! His hips were pressed against the barrel. He put his hands behind him and one of them closed on the hatchet that the kitchen helper had used to open the barrel.

Jackson swung the hatchet up then down. There was a sickening thud as it landed. The Deacon's dropped gun smacked on the hard packed earth in front of the barrel. The sound of a falling body followed the sound of the falling gun. Then there was no sound in the basement but Jackson's own breathing.

Keeping close to the wall, he felt his way to the door. He wanted to close the master switch and didn't dare. He knew that what he would see would make him sick again. Out in the basement, his trailing fingers touched Larry's camel's hair coat and hat. There was no longer any need to light the lights or strike a match to look for the Deacon's gun. There was a gun in the right-hand sash pocket of the topcoat.

Jackson felt his way to the stairs and climbed them. The key was in the door. He unlocked the door and found himself in a remembered small service areaway.

The club proper was almost as dark as the basement had been. The only light was a brilliant white spot shining on the red-haired girl who had grabbed him and called him darling. She was a pretty girl and well-formed. But unlike the little brunette strip teaser he had seen in the North Clark Street bar, the red-haired girl was enjoying what she was doing.

Her costume was utter simplicity — the charms with which nature had endowed her and a pair of high-heeled shoes.

Several waiters passed him. They glanced at and recognized the coat but not the man inside it.

Jackson walked back down the hall and looked through the glass in the swinging kitchen doors. Dave Brey was standing in the back door, looking out into the night. The front and side doors would be similarly guarded. Flip wasn't taking any chances. Not until the Deacon and Larry had made him talk.

One hand on the gun in his pocket, Jackson walked back down the hall and opened the door of Flip's office, the same office into which Olga had blundered. There was no one in the office. Jackson closed the door and crossed the hall and opened the door of his former dressing room.

From the row of expensive looking dresses in the closet and the pastel mink coat thrown carelessly across a well-used chaise longue, he decided it was the red-haired girl's dressing room now.

Jackson looked up, then down the hall to make certain he wasn't observed, then entered the dressing room and closed the door behind him.

16

INSIDE the dressing room, Jackson could still hear the music faintly. It pulsed through a sensuous routine, then rose to a crashing crescendo of suggestive drum beats, as the nude red-haired dancer went into her final bumps. A smattering of applause followed, the lack of enthusiasm not due to any disapproval of lewdness. It was merely that as far as sensuality was concerned, the jaded patrons of the Club Bali much preferred participation to observation.

Jackson wished he had a cigar. Success, he thought, was a funny thing. To achieve it a man had to work like hell. He had to know all the angles. All a pretty girl had to do was take off her clothes. If you could call doing a strip at the Club Bali success. As he remembered from hearing the girls talk, it was the after-hours that built up the bank account. The spotlight and dance floor were merely the means of displaying the merchandise.

He found a box of imported cigarettes in the litter of the dressing table and lighted one. The first puff tasted good. The second puff was more perfume than tobacco. The red-haired girl had obviously carried the box in her purse. He snuffed the cigarette and stood looking out the barred window.

His head and the side of his face throbbed. The clotted blood on the flesh wound the Deacon's last shot had burned across his thigh itched with persistent annoyance. He had just killed a man, possibly two men. Nothing as yet was solved or proven. He might still be killed. He was almost certain to take another beating. Still, in the entire past nightmare, only one fact stood out, a casual remark by the Deacon. Larry had asked about Thelma and the Deacon had said: *God knows where she is. I warned Flip against that broad. I knew that sooner or later she was going to cause us trouble. She wasn't 'happy' here, if you get what I mean. Then when Flip pulled that bonehead play of trying to get her to lay Pierce, well, pop went the weasel.*

Thelma wasn't 'happy' here. The thought warmed Jackson. Thelma's type of girl wouldn't be happy in a place like the Club Bali. She had simply gotten into something that was too big for her to cope with. When she'd had a chance to get out, she'd taken it. His bruised lips twisted in a smile. Olga wasn't a miniature edition of Thelma. The blonde singer was an adult version of Olga. He hoped, no matter how this thing turned out, he would have a chance to tell Thelma how much he thought of her. Well, loved her, too. Although it wasn't considered cricket in Club Bali circles for a man to love his wife.

I meant to, Hart, she'd told him.

Hart wiped sweat from his forehead with his left hand. He wished he hadn't thought of her that way. Still, after all, Thelma was his wife. He wondered where she was and why, weak as she must be, she had left the hospital.

Behind him, the door knob of the dressing room turned. The barred window was across the room and to the right of the door. His back still turned to the door, he gripped the butt of the gun in the slash pocket of the topcoat and moved his head slightly so he could see the door in the light-ringed mirror over the dressing shelf. Then the door opened and the red-haired girl, wearing a white silk dressing gown over the charms she had just displayed, stood in the doorway talking to Lex Haven, the current M.C. of the Club Bali.

She was still breathing heavily from her exertions. There was a fine film of perspiration on her face. "The bastards!" she told Haven. "I hope to Chris' they all get eczema or something even nastier on their gawdam dirty hands. Such snotty applause. An' I was good t'night, too."

"You were great Mildred," the M.C. lied. "It's just that this time of morning all the old bucks are so busy trying to get their dates to agree to go to a hotel, they don't appreciate art."

Art? Jackson felt his stomach turn over. The younger man reminded him of a seven year younger Hart Jackson, lying like hell, placating, anything, to keep the alleged talent and Flip Evans' current love happy.

The red-haired girl patted the M.C.'s cheek. "Thanks a lot, Lex. You're sweet." She added in a lower tone, "If Flip wasn't so gawdam jealous, you an' me would get together sometime."

The red-haired girl closed the door and stalked to the dressing table, the skirts of her white gown trailing behind her. Jackson had been right in the service hall. All she was wearing were shoes. There wasn't even the customary sop of a net brassiere or a jeweled G-string. Jackson couldn't help getting excited. He thought: You should put on that act at Stateville, baby. You'd have no complaint about the applause. Or should she? The generated heat would melt the walls.

The girl picked a lucite comb from

her dressing shelf and ran it through her hair. Then she saw the big man at the window and her face contorted with anger. "You damn fool," she whispered fiercely. "Get out of here, Larry. You know now jealous Flip is. What if — "

Then she realized that while she was looking at Larry's coat and hat, someone else was wearing them. Her over-red lips opened even wider, as if she were going to scream.

"Uh uh, Mildred," Jackson warned her. "You let out one peep and I'll tell Flip you invited me in here." He turned and faced her. "And there goes your pastel mink."

She closed her mouth then opened it again. "My gawd. You're the guy I kicked."

"That's right."

The girl looked worried. "You wouldn't would you?"

"I wouldn't what?"

"Tell Flip I invited you in here."

"That all depends," Jackson said.

In a half-hearted attempt at modesty,

the red-haired girl clutched the neck of her dressing gown together. The bottom three-fourths of it still gaped, leaving her embarrassingly nude where it mattered. She stopped being worried and became puzzled. "But you're supposed to be down in the basement."

"I was."

She scratched herself absently. "You got it straightened out, huh?"

"Yeah."

"But what are you doing with Larry's coat?"

"Let's say I borrowed it."

"Oh."

Jackson studied the girl's face. She was lewd and shrewd but dumb. He doubted if she knew why he had been taken to the basement or what they had hoped to learn from him. That was to be expected. Nine-tenths of the help and the talent at the Club Bali had no knowledge of the fat nightclub owner's extra-curricular activity. He hadn't when he had worked at the club. At least not at first. The red-haired girl had been told to call him darling then grab him. She had. But there, probably, her knowledge of the affair ended.

As if tardily realizing she was exposing herself, she lowered her hand and caught the two edges of her dressing gown at the waist. It helped some but not much. The top half fell open now. Her firm, young, pear-shaped breasts were as pretty as her legs. Jackson tried hard not to look at them.

"It all depends on what?" she asked him. "I mean, I said you wouldn't get me in trouble with Flip, anyway that's what I meant, by saying I invited you in here. And you said it all depends." She wet her lips with the tip of a pink tongue and somehow made the gesture suggestive. "What do you want of me?"

"Not what you're thinking," Jackson told her. "All I want is some information."

She looked disappointed. "Oh."

"What do you know about Alice Willard?"

The red-haired girl was smugly superior. "That little tart!"

258

"Even so. She's pretty?"

"Some men seem to think so."

"Where can I find her?"

"You can't."

"Why not?"

The girl released her dressing gown and began to comb her hair. "Because she's in Florida, that's why. Flip bought her a ticket and she flew down last night."

"Last night?"

"You heard me."

"You're positive?"

She continued to comb her hair. "Of course I am. You think I'm dumb or something? I drove out to the Cicero airport with Flip and the Deacon when they put her on the plane."

"I see."

"I guess I ought to know."

"Of course. But I thought she left with Fillmore Pierce three or four nights ago."

"You mean that old white-haired goat?"

"That's the one."

"Naw," the red-haired girl scoffed. "He wanted to marry Thelma. Him and Flip had a deal of some kind. The way I get it, it meant a lot of money for Flip. The old goat gave him some, even. Then Thelma wouldn't have any part of it. She — " She stopped combing her hair and bit at her lower lip instead of continuing what she had been about to say. Her eyes were worried. "Say, you *are* one of the boys, ain't you? You ain't no fly cop or nothing like that?"

"What did Larry tell you I was?"

"He said you were one of the stick men from up on the second floor and you'd been shaking down on the game and they were going to beat hell out of you." She continued, uncertain now, her eyes searching his face. "But you don't look like no gambler to me. Who are you?"

Jackson had lost interest in the girl. He knew what he wanted to know. Now if he could only figure some way to get out of the club.

"Who are you?" Mildred repeated.

"You ever read the newspapers, honey?" Jackson asked her.

She shook her red hair. "Naw. Just the funnies, Little Abner and Blondie, especially. And once in awhile Variety. So what do I care what happens in Moscow or maybe even in Omaha, South Dakota? I asked you a question. Who are you?"

There was a small French doll resting against the curve of the chaise longue. Jackson picked it up and suddenly the doll leaned forward and seemed to say, "If you're smart, honey, you'll keep your questions to yourself."

It was a mistake on Jackson's part. The red-haired girl dropped the comb to the floor and stood terrified. "I make you now. You're the guy who used to emcee here, the one all the girls are talking about, the one who had Thelma shot."

"So?" Jackson asked.

She took a step toward him and her white robe slipped down over her ivory satin shoulders. "So don't hurt me, please. I don't know nothing about

261

your quarrel with Flip. I just did what they told me. Honest."

Jackson backed away from her. "Okay. I'm not blaming you."

The girl didn't seem to hear him. Her robe slipped to the floor as she continued to advance. "Please don't hurt me."

"I don't intend to hurt you."

Her eyes kept searching his face. She ran her palms over her hair and pressed it together at the nape of her neck. Her breasts rose with the gesture. She wet her lips with her tongue again. "If you don't hurt me, I will."

Jackson stood in the corner where she had backed him. He'd never been less interested in a proposition. He was interested in what she hoped to gain by her offer. "You will what?"

She ran her tongue along her lips, slowly this time. "You know what I mean."

"Where?"

"Right here."

"When?"

"Right now." She turned away from

him. "Just wait till I lock the door."

Jackson caught one of her wrists. "It was a good try, baby. But if you think I'm going to let you open that door and scream your head off for Flip, you're crazy."

Instead of trying to pull away, she came into his arms and pressed herself against him. "I'm not going to scream, honest, honey," she lied. "I kinda like you." And then she did scream, clawing at his face and trying to wrestle him to the floor at the same time. "Help! Rape! Oh, someone, please help me," she screamed.

Jackson tried to push her away from him and draw his gun. The red-haired girl clung to his forearm with surprising strength, then thrusting one of her bare legs between his, she tripped him as he tried to break free. They fell heavily, with her partially on top of him, still screaming, "Rape! Help! Someone, please help me!"

Bare, powdered flesh smothered Jackson. He pushed the screaming girl off his face and managed to get to his feet before the door of the dressing room burst open and Dave Brey filled the opening with Flip looming large behind him.

Brey's gun was already in his hand. "Uh uh," he warned Jackson. "Hold it, just as you are."

In the instant that the door was open, Jackson caught a quick glimpse of a group of excited chorus girls and cooks and waiters. Then Brey and Flip entered the room. Evans slammed the door behind him and leaned against it.

The fat man's wattles were purple with anger. "How did you get out of that basement, you bastard? Okay. This cooks it!" He looked at Brey. "Well, don't just stand there looking at me. Think of something. McCreary may come back any minute. We've got to get him out of here and over to the penthouse. What did the Deacon find out? Did he find out where the kid is?"

Brey tried to speak and Evans continued

before he could. "Well, do something, you hear me? Get the Deacon and let's get this guy out of here."

Brey looked like he was going to be sick momentarily. His voice when he spoke was thick. "If you want the Deacon, go down and get him yourself. But he ain't going anywhere."

"What do you mean by that?"

"What I said. I just went down to the basement to see what was taking him and Larry so long and the Deacon ain't ever going nowhere again. Larry may make it, maybe not. But Jackson used a hatchet on the Deacon." Brey tried to repress a shudder and failed. "Right between the eyes."

The red-haired girl stood up, then stooped and picked her white robe from the floor and slipped her arms into it. "Chris', am I glad you guys came when you did."

Evans looked from Brey to her. "How come that Jackson came in here?"

She said, "He wanted a woman, I guess. He did his best to — well, you know what I mean."

Evans slapped her brutally. "To hell with that. A guy in the spot he's in isn't thinking about quail. He ask you any questions?"

The girl turned sullen-eyed. "Yes. He did."

"About what?"

"About Alice Willard."

"What about her?"

"He wanted to know when she went to Florida!"

"And what did you tell him?"

"Nothing," the red-haired girl lied. "I didn't tell him a thing. What do you think, I'm dumb or something?"

17

JACKSON stood drained of emotion. He'd never felt so futile, so frustrated. So now he knew, for all the good it was going to do him. Seemingly, nothing he did was right. Nothing he'd done since he'd left Stateville was right, with the exception of marrying Thelma and keeping Olga out of Flip's hands.

It was so easy to second guess. Instead of trying to be clever, he should have shot his way out of the club. In a radio or TV show, that was what he would have done. Unfortunately, in real life you had to play the cards as they fell. Then, too, if he'd tried to shoot his way out of the club, by now he'd probably be as dead as the Deacon.

He was an entertainer not a gunman. He could point a gun. He could pull a trigger. But at anything over a distance of ten feet, he doubted very much if he could hit the north end of Flip headed south.

Evans took a fat cigar from his pocket. "You positive?" he asked the girl. "I mean you're positive you didn't tell Jackson anything about Alice?"

She fluttered her mascaraed eyelashes at him. "Of course I am."

The nightclub owner slapped Jackson across the lips with the back of one of his fat hands. "Okay. Where did you hide that kid, Hart?"

Jackson suddenly was tired. He'd never been so tired. His body felt it had been pounded on for days. He doubted if he could take another beating. He considered telling Flip what he had done with Olga. If things had gone as he hoped they had, it shouldn't matter now. He tried to tell Flip and couldn't. His pride refused to allow him to make that concession to fear.

The French doll on the chaise longue answered for him. "Go to hell, you fat tub of guts."

"The guy is good," Mildred simpered.

"How does he do that?"

Her mental quotient, Jackson decided, was about on a par with Olga's, with Olga having a slight edge.

A moment of silence followed. Then Dave Brey asked, "So? What if McCreary has left a stake-out? How are we going to get him out of the club?"

Evans looked at Jackson, then at the red-haired girl. "Isn't that Larry's coat he's wearing?" he asked her.

"Also Larry's hat," Mildred said. "That's why I didn't scream sooner. I thought that he was Larry. Then when I asked him where he got 'em, he said he borrowed them."

"Get dressed," Evans told her.

"Whatever you say, darling," the girl answered. She took off the white robe and began to dress for the street as unconcerned as if she were alone in the dressing room.

Evans put the cigar he was holding between his lips and lighted it. The fragrant aroma of the tobacco and the shapely body of the girl added to

Jackson's torment. "We'll go out the side door," Evans told Brey between puffs. "McCreary has seen that coat before. He has also seen Mildred. And if the four of us just walk out like we haven't a care, the chances are, if there is a stake-out, he'll mistake Jackson for Larry. If we are stopped, so what? The cops don't want me."

"So far," Jackson needled him.

Evans continued doggedly. "After all, it's my word against the words of a seven-year-old kid."

His voice wasn't as confident as his words.

Brey put the gun he'd taken from Jackson into the left-hand pocket of his topcoat and thumbed the safety on, then thumbed it off the automatic he held in his right hand. "Even so, I'd feel a lot better if we could pick up both her and Thelma."

Evans patted at the film of perspiration on his face. "So would I," he admitted. He glanced at his diamond set wristwatch and flicked a switch on the wall. The dressing room immediately began to fill with music.

Jackson recognized it as the theme song of the Rounder's Lullaby. He'd heard it a hundred times in his cell, lying unable to sleep, staring up into the dark, listening to his small, muted and forbidden radio.

Lex Haven came on the air. "Heigh-ho and a merry-oh, all ye late stayers-up." The kid, Jackson thought, has a nice voice and a pleasing personality. He should go far, if Flip didn't manage to foul him up. The youthful M.C. continued, "This is Lex Haven, ye old sinful maestro of the glamorous Club Bali calling all sinners to our morning session of the Rounders' Lullaby. Fill up your glasses, boys. Kiss the girl in your arms — bring her to see us sometime."

The band playing softly behind him came in forte with a sweet liquorish stick man carrying the melody of an old blues arrangement.

Mildred slipped a dress over the pantyhose she'd put on, then pulled

271

the dress almost to her hips as she straightened the pantyhose waist. Jackson was wryly amused. He was on his way to take what could be a fatal beating and Flip's current girl friend was worried about her underwear.

"What if I put up a fuss?" he asked Evans.

The fat man was frank. "That's up to you, Hart. You can walk out or be carried out. I can't afford to fool with you any longer. I have to know where that kid is. If the cops get their hands on her, it could mean my ass."

The French doll on the chaise longue said, "Tch tch tch. And such a fat one, too."

Mildred was slipping her arms into the sleeves of the pastel mink. She giggled at the wise crack then looked guiltily at Evans. The fat man gave her a dirty look but refrained from speaking.

Dave Brey put his gun in the pocket of his topcoat. "All right. Let's go, Hart. You and me will go first. And no monkey business, understand? I'd just as soon slug you as not. Keep about half a step ahead of me."

There was no one in the hall now. The last show had gone on and the chorus line had gone home or elsewhere according to individual inclinations. The kitchen was closed for the night. Only the bar and the service bar were open.

"You know the way," Evans said. "And cut across the back of the band-stand. I'd rather have one of the muggle tooters recognize you than some drunk."

Jackson took a deep breath and did as he was told. Lex Haven was crooning into the mike. Several of the musicians glanced up, recognized Evans and Mildred and Brey and returned their attention to their instruments.

The mike into which Haven was crooning was invitingly close. Halfway across the dimly lighted dais, Jackson filled his lungs with air and made a break for it, with Dave close behind him swinging the barrel of his gun.

"You bastard," Brey breathed . "You bastard."

The gun barrel found Jackson's head when he was less than three feet from the microphone. He stumbled and would have fallen if Haven hadn't reached out and caught him.

"Thanks, Lex," Brey whispered. The gun was back in his topcoat again, its steel muzzle gouging into Jackson's spine. "Come on, let's go, pal," he said aloud. "Boy, have you got a snootful. You can hardly stand."

White-faced, watching the two men, Lex Haven continued to croon into the microphone.

Jackson stood, breathing hard, his nostrils fluted, his lips compressed in disappointment, mixed blood and perspiration trickling down the back of his neck. Then the pain of the gun muzzle boring into the small of his back acted as a counter-irritant and cleared his head. The gun gouged even deeper. With a last disappointed look at the microphone into which Haven was singing, he yielded to the pressure of the gun and walked back across the dais to where Flip and Mildred were waiting.

The fat man sighed with relief. "Nice work, Dave. For a moment I was afraid the big bastard was going to yip into that mike."

"He ran out of guts," Brey boasted. "I damn near caved in the back of his head." He drew the gun from his pocket again and looked at Jackson. "So what's the score now, chump? Do you want to walk or be carried?"

Jackson made his choice. "I'll walk."

He hadn't far to go. The side door of the Club Bali opened into an unlighted alley. The package room door of the forty-apartment building that Evans owned and on top of which he maintained a penthouse apartment was only a half-block down the alley.

The alley smelled of decaying garbage. Squealing rats scurried out of the way of the oddly assorted foursome. As far as Jackson could tell there was no stake-out in the alley. No one saw them descend the four stone stairs into the package room. Once safely inside, Evans wiped at the perspiration on his face with a silk handkerchief.

"Now I feel better," he admitted.

He led the way through the unlighted basement into a boiler room. The room smelled of steam. A red glow spilled out from the partly opened door of the ash pit.

The heavy footsteps of the men and the sharp clock of Mildred's spike heels on the concrete floor sounded unnaturally loud in Jackson's ears. Hell must be something like this, Jackson thought. He no longer felt any fear. Both his mind and his body were numb.

Evans unlocked the door in the back of the boiler room and stepped aside to allow Mildred and Brey and Jackson to precede him. Behind the door was a small cage and an elevator shaft that opened into Evans' apartment.

As Evans closed the door, he grunted, "You've ridden this old gray mare, eh, Hart?"

"That's right," Jackson admitted. "On the night you killed Helene and tried to pin it on my kid brother."

There was a dim light in the steel top of the cage. Evans looked at Jackson reproachfully. "Now you shouldn't ought to talk like that, pal. Especially in front of Milly. It might give the broad ideas." Evans looked at the red-haired girl. "And if there's anything I hate worse than a wise guy, it's a broad who thinks she has something on me."

The red-haired girl's smile was forced. "No. Please, Flip. Don't look at me that way. I never even heard what he said. I mean I didn't pay no attention."

The cage creaked slowly upward. Few people knew of its existence. Unless he was pressed for time or wanted to leave or enter the building without being seen, Evans seldom used it. Ordinarily he used the regular tower elevator.

The penthouse hadn't changed since Jackson had seen it last. It was a decorator's nightmare. There was too much of everything. It violated all good taste. It had cost Flip Evans a fortune to furnish it but the only beautiful thing about it was the view of the city and Lake Michigan that it afforded from the landscaped terraces on the east and west sides.

Evans took off his coat and called, "Ramon."

There was no answer. He called again then went in search of his missing houseboy. There was a thoughtful look in his eyes as he returned to the living room. "That's funny."

"What's funny?" Brey asked.

Evans said, "Ramon isn't in his room. His bed hasn't been slept in. And I distinctly remember telling him not to go out tonight." He took off his suit coat, folded it neatly and laid it on a chrome and white leather love seat. "Some days are like this, I guess. I'll work that yellow bastard over plenty in the morning."

It was hot in the penthouse with the big French windows to the terrace closed. As he untied his black bow tie and took off his shirt and collar, Evans added, "Open a couple of them windows, Dave."

Brey did as he was told and a broom of crisp, fresh air swept the apartment. As he unlocked a third window he asked, "But what if someone hears him yell?"

Evans laid his shirt on top of his coat. "They won't. Not this high." A smug smile twisted his fat lips as he looked at Mildred. "You'd be surprised at the yelling and screaming that's gone on in this joint, some of it from dames who didn't have sense enough to know on which side their bread was buttered."

Mildred sat on an ornate Oriental hassock, her smile even more forced than it had been in the elevator cage. "Don't look at me like that, darling. Didn't I scream as soon as I recognized the guy?"

"Before or after he did it to you?"

"Don't be like that, Flip."

Evans loosened his belt a notch. "Not that it particularly matters. Broads are a dime a dozen. Just keep your mouth shut about what you're going to see, understand."

The red-haired girl squirmed like a bitch cocker puppy eager to please her master. "Of course, I un'erstand. An' the cops could kill me before I would open my mouth." She stroked the pastel mink. "I never had it so good as I have it with you, lover boy."

Jackson shifted his weight from one foot to the other. It made him feel unclean just listening to them. The one thing he regretted was not having been able to kill Flip. The fat nightclub owner befouled everything he touched.

He looked from the frightened girl to Evans. Stripped to the waist the fat man didn't look so fat. There were still corded muscles under his blubber. His forearms and biceps still bulged. He could still tear a telephone book in two or crush a man's skull with one blow. The next few minutes weren't going to be very pleasant.

Evans padded across the thick nap of the burgundy carpet and tapped on Jacksons' chest with a stubby fore finger, like he was knocking on a door. "Now, look, Hart." What followed was a flat statement. "I'm not the law. I'm not a punk like either Larry or the Deacon. The name is Evans."

"So?"

"Where's Olga?"

"And if I refuse to tell you?"

The fat man doubled a pudgy hand into a fist, then lowered the fist to his side as a feminine voice said, "I *thought* I heard voices in here."

Jackson turned slowly, with a great effort of will. Thelma was standing in the open doorway of the bedroom.

"Well, I'll be godammed," Brey said.

The blonde girl looked pale and weak but even prettier than she had the last time Jackson had seen her. Her eyes were slightly puffed as if she had been sleeping or crying, but she was carefully made up. Her firm high breasts filled the jacket of a smart beige pants suit. A wide headband of the same color was tied around her straw-colored hair. A natural leather shoulder bag weighted one small shoulder. Her smile was the smile of a woman who wanted to look her best.

"How long you been in there?" Evans asked.

Thelma said, "Since shortly after I escaped from the hospital." her smile turned wry. "I have a key, remember?"

Evans' bare chest expanded. "You crawled back, eh?"

The blonde girl was apologetic. "I — I guess you could call it that."

"Why?"

Thelma was still so weak she had to cling to the jamb of the door to stand. She looked at Jackson then away. Her voice continued small. "It could be that I realized on which side my bread is buttered." Her slim fingers fondled the wilted three-orchid corsage on her shoulder. Her eyes turned suspiciously bright. "On the other hand, does a girl need a reason when she realizes she is in love with a guy, that she has to be with him, no matter what?"

18

EVANS was very well pleased with Evans. "How's that, eh?" he asked Dave Brey. "When I drive a nail in a plank it stays driven." He returned his attention to Thelma. "Okay. So you're back. It can just be I'll let you stay."

"Thank you," Thelma said simply.

The red-haired girl stood up. "Now, wait just a minute, you two."

"Sit down," said Evans.

The red-haired girl sat down.

Evans looked back at Thelma. "And you take off them orchids. If you're leveling with me, what's the idea of wearing them?"

Her hands trembling from weakness, Thelma unpinned the orchids and laid them carefully on a brass coffee table. "I'm sorry if I shouldn't have worn them. But I saw them lying on the dining room table. And I — I just wanted to look pretty."

"For the guy you love, huh?"

"Yes."

Evans ran a fat palm over his sleek black hair. His smile was smug. "By God, I tell you, Dave. When I make 'em they stay made."

Brey didn't seem so certain.

Evans returned his attention to Jackson. "Not that this changes anything for you." He slapped Jackson first with his palm, then with the back of his hand. "You're still going out of here in a laundry sack."

Jackson took a deep breath. "Uh uh."

"Why not?"

Jackson looked at Thelma a long moment, then back at the fat man. "You don't dare, Flip. You're whistling in the dark."

"What do you mean by that?"

"You don't dare to kill me."

"Why don't I?"

"Because you have to know where that kid is. Because if McCreary gets his hands on Olga and can get her to talk, he'll put two and two together."

"And come up with what?"

"Fillmore Pierce."

"Pierce is in Florida."

"You're positive?"

"I'm positive."

"How come?" Jackson asked quietly. "Did Alice Willard carry his cut-up body in her suitcase when you and the Deacon put her on that plane last night, so she could arrange with one of your Miami connections to phone Pierce's lawyers pretending he was Pierce?"

Evans walked over to the hassock on which the red-haired girl was sitting. "I thought you didn't talk."

The girl scowled at Thelma. "I didn'. I didn' say a word, so help me gawhd. But if I'd a knowed you was goin' to take up with this little blonde bitch again — "

The fat man slapped her off the hassock. "Shut up."

Thelma helped Mildred to her feet and led her to a fragile looking gold Louis XIVth chair. "Don't cry honey. You get used to it — in time. The slapping around is like the pastel mink. It comes with the bed and board. I know. I wore it myself for six months."

The red-haired girl ran the back of her hand under her nose as she sobbed, "Who's crying?"

Evans turned back to Jackson. "Okay. So I killed Pierce. So what? It wasn't my fault. It was Thelma's."

"Thelma's?"

"Yeah."

"How so?"

"Pierce was nuts about her. He wanted to marry her. So I took fifty grand to arrange it. Then she wouldn't go through with the deal and he wanted his money back."

"So you and Pierce quarreled and you killed him."

"Prove it. My saying so doesn't mean a thing." Evans boasted, "And I'd have gotten away with it clean if it hadn't been for Olga. How was I to know the brat was in the office? I damn near died when I turned around and seen her standing there holding that damned stuffed rabbit."

"You're talking too much, Flip," Brey said.

The nightclub owner shrugged. "Hart ain't going nowhere. Yes, sir. I damn near died when I seen her. I didn't even know Thelma had a kid sister."

Jackson said quietly, "But she has. And if she hadn't grabbed up Olga and run, both of them would probably have left the Club Bali in the same laundry truck with Pierce."

"Ha," Evans said.

Jackson continued, "Or, however his body left the club, if it did. That's why Thelma looked me up. She knew I had reason to hate you. She knew I was supposed to be a right guy. She was afraid to go to the police. She knows how much pull you have. She knows how witnesses against you have a habit of disappearing. That's why she was willing to give herself to me and insure her life in my favor. She knew you would probably try to kill her as you did."

Evans patted the blonde girl with his eyes. "That was a mistake. I see that now. From now on, me and Thelma are going to get along fine."

Jackson ignored him. "She also knew that if I could, I would take care of Olga."

Evans was amused. "So that would seem to sum it up. Sure I killed Pierce. When I couldn't deliver Thelma and wouldn't give him his money back, the old goat called me a pimp. He was going to have me pinched for running a confidence game. And with the money he had behind him, he could have done it, too." Evans picked a fat cigar from a humidor and lighted it. The smell of the fragrant Havana made Jackson's taste buds water. Evans continued, amused, "So you came back to Chicago to kill me, eh, Hart? A shame you ran into this other thing. You're tough. You got nerve. You might have gotten away with it. By the way, how's Jerry?"

"He's dead," Jackson told him. "Shot down over Vietnam, flying a jet."

The fat man chuckled. "Well, that should learn him to let other men's broads alone. I did my best to send the little punk up for murder. I thought I was damn clever. I killed Helene Adele in such a way he couldn't help but take the fall. And he'd have done it, too, if it hadn't been for you. So what's your grudge against me? If you were fool enough to step in and take the rap, that's skin off your nose, not mine."

Jackson looked out of one of the tall French windows opening onto the set-back terrace. It was surprising, even this high up, how much a man could see. He thought: The poet who said, 'Though every prospect pleases and only man is vile,' is wrong. Only some men are vile. He said aloud, "You still can't get away with it, Flip. Remember, you still have Olga to consider."

"To hell with her," Evans patted Thelma again, with a fat hand this time. "It doesn't matter, now Thelma realizes how much she loves me, now she's come back to me. The kid will do whatever Thelma tells her to do. And even if she should talk, with Thelma to back me, all I have to say is that Olga is lying."

Brey patted at the perspiration on his face, relieved. "We came out better than we thought we would," he admitted. "But what are we going to do about Jackson?"

Evans rolled the cigar between his fat lips. "We knock him off and take him downstairs. If the fire box of the furnace is big enough to hold Fillmore Pierce, it's big enough to hold him." He spoke with no more compunction than if he had been about to pole an ox. "Give me that other gun, the one he took off Larry, and I'll do it."

The fat man took a step toward Brey and stopped short as Thelma said, "I wouldn't, Flip."

"You wouldn't what?"

Thelma told him. "Even look dirty at Jackson." Her voice continued small but it was cold and somehow deadly.

The fat man looked over one bare

shoulder and the blood drained slowly from his face. The blonde girl had taken a small but businesslike looking automatic from her shoulder bag. The safety was off. The nuzzle was leveled at the small of his back. "What's the idea?" he asked thickly.

Her eyes bright with tears again. Thelma said, "I told you when I came in. Maybe I haven't been smart. Maybe I haven't been good. I've done a lot of things of which I am ashamed, of which I'll always be ashamed. But a long time ago when I was a kid, I dreamed I'd fall in love with a right guy, the kind of a man of whom a girl could be proud. And I damn near died there in the hospital when the nurse told me that Hart had showed up, carrying Olga and her rabbit. That's why I escaped. To get to him, thinking maybe I could help." Tears streamed down her cheeks. "But like I told you before, does a girl have to have reasons when she realizes she's in love with a guy, that nothing else matters, that she has to be with him, no matter what?"

Evans turned and faced her. "Why, you dirty, double-crossing little bitch." He walked back toward her slowly. "And me thinking you loved me. Go ahead. Pull the trigger of that peashooter. I'll take it away from you and you'll be surprised where I'll put it."

Still weak and faint, the blonde girl swayed like a reed in a high wind. The gun was too heavy for her hand. It sagged.

"Hold it a minute, Flip," Brey advised. "She's going to faint."

The fat man took another step toward Thelma and the red-haired girl got to her feet and put her arm around Thelma's waist. She, too, was crying. "You leave her alone, ya fat tub of guts," she warned Evans. "I might have knowed what kind of a guy ya was." She wriggled out of the pastel mink and let it hang by the arm supporting Thelma. "An' while you're putting things, ya can put your gawdam fur coat where it tickles you the most. When ya drive a nail in a plank it stays driven. Ha!"

Evans turned white at the insult to his manhood.

He took another step and Jackson stepped in between him and the two girls. "Uh uh, Flip. This is it. All good things have to end some time."

"The hell you say," the fat man said. He lifted a massive fist to pole Jackson and a voice seeming to come from one of the tall French windows opening onto the set-back warned him: "Hold it right there, Evans. This is the Law."

The fat man didn't bother to look behind him. "And don't try to give me none of that crappy throwing your voice stuff." Evans held a hand behind him. "Give me that gun I asked you for, Dave."

Brey failed to answer and Evans turned to see why. His hands raised shoulder high, Brey stood facing the wall with Sergeant Nelson's gun in the small of his back.

It was a regulation gun matching the one in Lieutenant McCreary's hand and, for that matter, in the hands of the cold-eyed men moving in from the set-back terrace.

Evans' knees refused to hold him. He sat on the edge of the white leather and chrome love seat. "How long you guys been out there?"

"Long enough," McCreary assured him. "Ever since Mrs. Jackson let us in with her key." McCreary started a small grin and it spread all over his face. "If you only know how I love you, Flip."

"Love me?" the fat man puzzled.

"Yeah," Lieutenant McCreary told him. "You're a new Buick, eight hundred more a year and an up-in-rank to me."

Evans accused. "You knew. You knew when you were at the club. Jackson sent Olga to you."

"That's right," McCreary agreed. "And damn smart of him, too. The kid wouldn't talk to me. She'd promised her sister not to. But you know how women are when they get together. And she spilled the whole thing to my seven-year-old daughter, Bunny; all about how the bad fat man and the white-haired man shouted dirty words at each other and then the bad fat man shooted the white-haired man and he fell down and his face was all bloody. Could I help it if I happened to be listening?"

"You bastards, you bastards," the fat man said without heat. He glanced at the hall door of the penthouse.

"I wouldn't try it if I were you, Flip," McCreary said. "In the first place I can't think of anything I'd rather do than shoot you. In the second place there are more police and police cars milling around the building than Irishmen in a St. Patrick's day parade."

"It got out, then?" Jackson asked.

Lieutenant McCreary nodded. "And were a lot of milkmen and barmen surprised when, right along with Lex Haven's Rounders' Lullaby, they hear a man whispering in the mike, 'This is Hart Jackson, wanted for attempted murder, speaking. Call the nearest policeman. Hurry. I am on the bandstand of the Club Bali. But I won't be here long. Tell the police to go to Flip Evans' penthouse.'"

Evans fat jowls turned an apoplectic purple. "Damn you, Hart, I was watching you. You didn't even move your lips."

Jackson looked at him wide-eyed. "A ventriloquist is supposed to move his lips?"

Insane with fear, the fat man hurled himself at Jackson, his big fists thudding like sledges. Jackson met the rush with a hard right to Evans' jaw and a short left to his stomach. One of the detectives started to interfere and Lieutenant McCreary shook his head.

"Uh, uh," he told the detective. "So far the party has been on Jackson. Let him have his piece of cake."

The two men were equally matched. Jackson had his hate. Evans was insane with fear. For five minutes there was no sound but the smack of fists on flesh and the grunts and hoarse breathing of the two big men. Then Jackson knocked Evans from his feet and was sitting straddling him doing a good job of beating the fat man's face to a bloody pulp when Lieutenant McCreary stopped the fight.

"Okay. That's all, fellow," McCreary said. He nodded to one of his squad and together they pulled Jackson away from the prostrate fat man. "You've softened him up fine. Thanks a lot. We'll take over from here."

Sucking great gasps of air into his lungs, Jackson tried to shake off their hands. "I came to Chicago to kill him."

"So?" McCreary asked. "What are you bitching about? You did what you came back to do." He touched the weeping fat man with his foot. "True, he isn't quite dead yet. But what with Flip's oral confession as recorded by a police stenographer and on tape and all of the boys and girls, including Dave Brey there, who are going to turn canary, the Sovereign State of Illinois will take care of the matter for you." McCreary thought a moment. "Allowing for his trial and an appeal, I'd say about six months from now."

Jackson wiped the sweat from his forehead with the sleeve of his borrowed topcoat. The feel of the cloth made him sick. He wanted to look at Thelma and didn't dare. "There's one other little matter, lieutenant," he said, quietly.

"What?"

"I did seven years on a bad rap, but you've got a live one on me now. There is one, possibly two dead men in the basement of the club."

"Who?"

"The Deacon and a hood called Larry."

"Who killed them?"

"I did."

"And what were they doing when they were killed?"

"Trying to kill me."

Lieutenant McCreary explained, as if he might be explaining to Olga. In words of one syllable. "That is what we of the law call just-i-fi-a-ble hom-i-cide." He slapped Jackson's shoulder. "Sure. We'll have to take you to the Bureau. We may even have to hold you overnight." His small grin spread all over his face again. "But all you have to worry about is how to raise enough dough to go on a honeymoon. And if you can't raise it, by God, I'll lend it to you." He pushed Jackson away from him. "Now, go on. Get out of my hair while I tell the press what a smart detective I am. Who knows? I might even get an inspectorship out of this. The whole Department has been trying to get Evans for years."

Still wiping his face, Jackson walked slowly across the room to where Thelma was waiting for him. Her eyes were bright with tears again. She'd repinned his orchids on her shoulder. It was a pity, Jackson thought, that anything so beautiful should wilt.

They stood a moment looking at each other, neither quite certain what to say. Then Thelma said. "They stopped the messenger, but I — I found the flowers when I got here. And — the card signed, 'The Boy Friend, Peter Rabbit and Olga.'"

It was an effort for Jackson to speak. "She's all right?"

Thelma nodded. "Mm-hmm. She and Lieutenant McCreary's girl, Bunny, should be sound asleep." The tears in the blonde girl's eyes spilled over and ran down her cheeks. "And Lieutenant McCreary said that after she'd told Bunny about what happened at the club, all she could talk about was the wonderful new big brother she had."

Jackson touched the girl's wet cheeks with the finger tips of one hand. "You're crying, honey."

Thelma met his eyes. "Women usually cry when they're happy."

"And you're happy now?"

"That's up to you." Thelma smiled.

"I love you, honey," Jackson said quietly.

The blonde girl's eyes shone even brighter. "Now I'm happy."

Then she was in Jackson's arms, the wilted orchids crushed between them.

"My darling, my darling," Thelma whispered.

The red-haired strip teaser stood so as to shield them as much as she could then ran the back of her hand under her nose as she looked at the grinning detectives and said, "All right. All right, you wise guys. Get on with your detectin'. What was ya, born on a farm or somethin'? Didn't ya never see a man kiss his wife before?"

THE END

A FOOT IN THE GRAVE
Bruce Marshall

About to be imprisoned and tortured in Buenos Aires, John Smith escapes, only to become involved in an aeroplane hijacking.

DEAD TROUBLE
Martin Carroll

Trespassing brought Jennifer Denning more than she bargained for. She was totally unprepared for the violence which was to lie in her path.

HOURS TO KILL
Ursula Curtiss

Margaret went to New Mexico to look after her sick sister's rented house and felt a sharp edge of fear when the absent landlady arrived.

THE DEATH OF ABBE DIDIER
Richard Grayson

Inspector Gautier of the Sûreté investigates three crimes which are strangely connected.

NIGHTMARE TIME
Hugh Pentecost

Have the missing major and his wife met with foul play somewhere in the Beaumont Hotel, or is their disappearance a carefully planned step in an act of treason?

BLOOD WILL OUT
Margaret Carr

Why was the manor house so oddly familiar to Elinor Howard? Who would have guessed that a Sunday School outing could lead to murder?

THE DRACULA MURDERS
Philip Daniels

The Horror Ball was interrupted by a spectral figure who warned the merrymakers they were tampering with the unknown.

THE LADIES
OF LAMBTON GREEN
Liza Shepherd

Why did murdered Robin Colquhoun's picture pose such a threat to the ladies of Lambton Green?

CARNABY
AND THE GAOLBREAKERS
Peter N. Walker

Detective Sergeant James Aloysius Carnaby-King is sent to prison as bait. When he joins in an escape he is thrown headfirst into a vicious murder hunt.

MUD IN HIS EYE
Gerald Hammond

The harbourmaster's body is found mangled beneath Major Smyle's yacht. What is the sinister significance of the illicit oysters?

THE SCAVENGERS
Bill Knox

Among the masses of struggling fish in the *Tecta*'s nets was a larger, darker, ominously motionless form . . . the body of a skin diver.

DEATH IN ARCADY
Stella Phillips

Detective Inspector Matthew Furnival works unofficially with the local police when a brutal murder takes place in a caravan camp.

STORM CENTRE
Douglas Clark

Detective Chief Superintendent Masters, temporarily lecturing in a police staff college, finds there's more to the job than a few weeks relaxation in a rural setting.

THE MANUSCRIPT MURDERS
Roy Harley Lewis

Antiquarian bookseller Matthew Coll, acquires a rare 16th century manuscript. But when the Dutch professor who had discovered the journal is murdered, Coll begins to doubt its authenticity.

SHARENDEL
Margaret Carr

Ruth didn't want all that money. And she didn't want Aunt Cass to die. But at Sharendel things looked different. She began to wonder if she had a split personality.

MURDER TO BURN
Laurie Mantell

Sergeants Steven Arrow and Lance Brendon, of the New Zealand police force, come upon a woman's body in the water. When the dead woman is identified they begin to realise that they are investigating a complex fraud.

YOU CAN HELP ME
Maisie Birmingham

Whilst running the Citizens' Advice Bureau, Kate Weatherley is attacked with no apparent motive. Then the body of one of her clients is found in her room.

DAGGERS DRAWN
Margaret Carr

Stacey Manston was the kind of girl who could take most things in her stride, but three murders were something different . . .

THE MONTMARTRE MURDERS
Richard Grayson

Inspector Gautier of Sûreté investigates the disappearance of artist Théo, the heir to a fortune.

GRIZZLY TRAIL
Gwen Moffat

Miss Pink, alone in the Rockies, helps in a search for missing hikers, solves two cruel murders and has the most terrifying experience of her life when she meets a grizzly bear!

BLINDMAN'S BLUFF
Margaret Carr

Kate Deverill had considered suicide. It was one way out — and preferable to being murdered.

BEGOTTEN MURDER
Martin Carroll

When Susan Phillips joined her aunt on a voyage of 12,000 miles from her home in Melbourne, she little knew their arrival would germinate the seeds of murder planted long ago.

WHO'S THE TARGET?
Margaret Carr

Three people whom Abby could identify as her parents' murderers wanted her dead, but she decided that maybe Jason could have been the target.

THE LOOSE SCREW
Gerald Hammond

After a motor smash, Beau Pepys and his cousin Jacqueline, her fiancé and dotty mother, suspect that someone had prearranged the death of their friend. But who, and why?

CASE WITH THREE HUSBANDS
Margaret Erskine

Was it a ghost of one of Rose Bonner's late husbands that gave her old Aunt Agatha such a terrible shock and then murdered her in her bed?

THE END OF THE RUNNING
Alan Evans

Lang continued to push the men and children on and on. Behind them were the men who were hunting them down, waiting for the first signs of exhaustion before they pounced.

CARNABY AND THE HIJACKERS
Peter N. Walker

When Commander Pigeon assigns Detective Sergeant Carnaby-King to prevent a raid on a bullion-carrying passenger train, he knows that there are traitors in high positions.

TREAD WARILY AT MIDNIGHT
Margaret Carr

If Joanna Morse hadn't been so hasty she wouldn't have been involved in the accident.

TOO BEAUTIFUL TO DIE
Martin Carroll

There was a grave in the churchyard to prove Elizabeth Weston was dead. Alive, she presented a problem. Dead, she could be forgotten. Then, in the eighth year of her death she came back. She was beautiful, but she had to die.

IN COLD PURSUIT
Ursula Curtiss

In Mexico, Mary and her cousin Jenny each encounter strange men, but neither of them realises that one of these men is obsessed with revenge and murder. But which one?